Loreto N. Gonzales Jr.

I0621589

Sacred
SILENCE

Lighthouse Publications

ISBN: 978-0-578-22982-9

PRINTED IN THE UNITED STATES OF AMERICA

In gratitude for my mother, Mrs. Carmen N. Gonzales
who celebrated her 100th birthday on May 17, 2019

1

"Father Sal Galvez, we are removing you from St. Barnabas parish," Bishop Lucio Soller said at our meeting in his office on March 26, 2014. Soller was the bishop in charge of the assignments of priests serving in the Archdiocese of Los Arboles in Southern California. In 2014, a population of approximately three million Roman Catholics lived within the jurisdiction of the Archdiocese of Los Arboles, whose spiritual head was Archbishop Joshua Fernandez. A hundred fifty parishes located in eighty cities, geographically divided into four pastoral regions, belonged to the archdiocese. Bishop Soller, the regional bishop of San Pio Pastoral Region, served under Archbishop Fernandez. St. Barnabas parish in Long Branch was one of the parishes in the San Pio Pastoral Region.

The day before, I took a call from Soller's secretary informing me that her boss wanted to see me. I asked what it was about. She said she didn't know. I wished I knew. Meetings tend to be productive when scheduled well in advance; agenda, well prepared. I learned this practical wisdom from Good Leaders, Good Shepherds Leadership Institute, which I recently completed. I agreed to be at the meeting in spite of the one-day notice, and I braced myself for an ambush.

Soller was seated on a leather chair behind his lacquered mahogany desk. He was dressed in black suit, black shirt with Roman collar, and black pants - the customary business attire of bishops. Except for the Roman collar and the pectoral cross, the chain hanging around his neck and the crucifix resting in the left black shirt pocket, he pretty much resembled Tommy Lee Jones in the *Men in Black* movie. I took the seat in front of his desk. I was not at ease. I didn't know what to expect. I wore the ordinary attire of diocesan priests—black pants and a black shirt with the Roman collar.

"Why?" I asked, feeling the pain as if punched in the stomach. I looked straight into Soller's dark brown eyes, then to the large crucifix hanging on the wall behind his chair, flanked by the framed photographs of Pope Francis and Archbishop Fernandez.

"Upon my recommendation, Archbishop Fernandez decided to end your term as pastor of St. Barnabas parish effective this coming April 1st."

"In five days, I'm out?" was my follow-up question. I stood up to make a point, "I have been pastor of St. Barnabas parish for more than ten years."

Soller stood up too, as if jacked up by the tensile strength of authority. Standing erect, he appeared much taller than he was, taller than an average Filipino. He first looked to the right side wall on which hung his bishop installation photo taken at Holy Angels, the cathedral church of the Archdiocese of Los Arboles. Then he turned to the left. Following his gaze, I took notice of an amalgam of framed photos of beautiful landscapes and beaches in the Philippines, the country where he was born, educated, and ordained a priest. He bent his head downward to meet my eyes. The fire of his eyeballs burned through my eyeglasses.

"Yes," he confirmed. He then reached over his desk to hand me the letter.

"It's heartless!" I exclaimed, inhaling a large dose of oxygen. I exhaled as I opened the envelope to read the first part of the letter, which bore his signature. It stated, *"Our record shows that you have exercised poor administration of the temporal goods of the parish. Such being the case, you have not done your share in helping the archdiocese pay the court-ordered four hundred million dollars settlement to the clergy sexual abuse victims."* Soller's letter further stated that I was to make arrangements to move to another residence in a location outside of the San Pio Pastoral Region, outside of his jurisdiction.

"Something's wrong here," I blurted out. "You should have sent me a notice at least a year ago."

"The archdiocese is under pressure from Los Angeles County Superior Court. The banks from which the archdiocese loaned the initial settlement money are flooding us with delinquent bills."

Soller sat down and tapped his fingers on the desk. "You are welcome to apply to be a pastor again at a later time." He opened the top drawer of his desk and fished out a calling card. "Dr. Charles Stein is a psychotherapist on call for the archdiocese," Soller said as he handed me the card. I took the card, only to read the address and telephone number listed on it. "See him for at least a couple of sessions," Soller instructed me. "Hopefully, after that, good fortune smiles in your favor."

"I'm seeing nothing but layers of contradictions on your face," I retorted. I tore up the card and tossed the pieces into the air.

"I am informing you now," the overreacting Soller said. "Canon Law states that your current term of office ends now." He pointed to the letter he just handed me. "It's in writing. In *that* letter."

"But it's *your* letter," I objected. "Where's the official letter from Archbishop Fernandez stating my removal? As practiced in the past, the archbishop's signature makes official priests' appointments."

Soller slammed his hands on the desk. *"I* speak for the archbishop.

My letter serves as the official word on his behalf," he declared. "Take it or leave it." Just like a judge at court, he delivered me the verdict. "Your removal is final." His voice rose to a high pitch. "And without undue delay."

"This is outrageous!" I cried out, deeply offended, wanting to vomit out my entire intestines.

2

The first time I got connected with St. Barnabas parish was on the week before Easter in 2004. That afternoon, I received a call from Archbishop Patrick O'Malley, who was then the archbishop of the Archdiocese of Los Arboles. He offered me the pastorate of St. Barnabas to succeed the former pastor who passed away the previous year. I was then finishing my twelfth year of pastorate at Holy Trinity in Alta Vista and was due for a new assignment.

That same afternoon, I visited St. Barnabas Church. As I stood in front of its façade, the gold-plated inscription, *To the Glory of God in honor of St. Barnabas*, impressed me. Its message clearly conveyed to me that the mission and purpose of the parish were to worship and glorify God in the tradition of St. Barnabas.

The church of St. Barnabas was built in 1951, the very same year I was born in the town of Madya-as, on the island of Panay in Central Philippines. Before I was born, my parents had two girls in a row. My mom wondered whether she would ever have a boy. Without telling my dad, she went to the church in the nearby town, stood in front of the statue of St. Joseph, and conversed with him. "St. Joseph, spouse of Mary, foster father of Jesus, father of the universal church, can we make a deal?" My mom spelled the terms out. "If you give me a boy, I'll see to it that he'll be a priest." St. Joseph didn't say a word. My mom was disappointed.

In due time, however, a year later, I was born, six days before the feast day of St. Joseph, which was universally celebrated by the Catholic Church on March 19th. My mom believed that I was the answer to her prayer. She was convinced that St. Joseph took the deal literally—only one boy. After me, all five subsequent siblings were girls.

As a kid growing up in a small town, after a few hours of fishing with an improvised bamboo fishing rod, I used to lie on my back in a small wooden boat floating aimlessly in the pond. I let the light breeze drift me to different corners of the pond. The wooden boat seemed much larger; the light breeze, surprisingly, powerful enough to steer it. I felt humbled.

My dad had left an indelible imprint on my boyhood. He wanted me to be a soldier in the tradition of the U.S. military. He served in the U.S. Navy during World War II as a mess officer and sacristan to Catholic chaplains. He was once stationed in Guadalcanal where one of the fiercest battles in the Pacific happened. I fondly remember him taking me to the movies about World War II battles. One that had stuck in my mind was *Sands of Iwo Jima*.

At ten, pretending to be a soldier, crouching over one of the hills in my hometown, imagining the enemy on the other side, I heard a voice say, "You're not going to make it. You're too short and small. You can't even carry a rifle." The voice was discouraging.

But my mom's voice was never discouraging. She explained to me that cruets, chalices, and censers used during church services were not as heavy as rifles. She made sure that I turned my attention to serving masses in our parish church at the earliest time. I complained to her that the altar boys' responses in Latin were more than I could take. Even harder to take was the parish priest's order for me to memorize the *Confiteor, Gloria,* and the *Credo* in one month, or else, the parish priest challenged me, I couldn't be an altar boy.

I told my mom about the unrealistic expectations of our parish priest. Realizing the difficult situation I was in, she told me of her dream ...

There we were, seated on one of the pews in our parish church attending Good Friday service that evening. As I watched the priest repeatedly slicing the flesh off the crucified body of Jesus with a sharp knife, I fell on my knees in reverence. I told you to kneel too, but you refused to. Instead, you looked away and told me that you could not stand seeing blood. In tears, you said, "Mama, I'm scared." Then, you walked away and disappeared in the darkness of the night. From then on I kept praying to Our Lady of Guadalupe to bring you home.

A soldier or a priest? I was in a crucible. To be molded to raise a rifle or to raise a chalice? On one hand, my mother was bent on keeping her promise to St. Joseph. On the other hand, my father argued with her, "Sal is our only boy. Who's going to keep on the family name?"

At twelve, I entered high school seminary that was located in the neighboring province. In my first year of high school in the seminary, in our class of forty-three, more than half had academic honors. The seminary rector asked me about my highest academic honor in grade school. For fear of being left behind (only twenty-three of us made it to sophomore year), I asserted, "Best in Attendance."

Before the end of that school year, in the month of April, which was the usual month for ordination to the priesthood, I admired how beautifully a newly ordained priest sang parts of his first mass (*canta misa*). Much as I admired him, I trembled at the thought that when the time came to say my first mass, would I be that good? The day after, in the seminary chapel, I knelt before the statue of the Blessed

Virgin Mary and said a desperate prayer, "Blessed Mother, if you really want me to be a priest, help me pass my music class." Something did happen. After the Vatican II Council, newly ordained priests were not required to sing at their first masses any longer.

In 1972, Ferdinand Marcos placed the Philippines under martial law. During the years of martial law, seminarians were challenged to think twice before they continued with priestly formation. They knew about the widening rift between the church and the government. Seminaries suspected of being subversive institutions were placed under surveillance by government agencies. Saul Alinsky's *Rules for the Radicals*, and Paulo Freire's *Pedagogy of the Oppressed*, both books promoting liberation theology, were on the government censors' list. Priests were put in jail; some, executed. The military closely monitored parish churches. Parishioners were too scared to speak publicly against the Marcos dictatorship. Like many other young people of my age, I was scared too. I was scared for my future. I believed, though, that God had a way of allaying my fear because I heard His voice, "To whomever I send you, you shall go; whatever I command you, you shall speak. Have no fear before them because I am with you to deliver you." (Jer. 1:7--8)

In June 1973, after I graduated from college seminary, I received a letter from the U.S. Embassy mandating me to immigrate to the U.S. I was born an American citizen by my father's American citizenship, *jus sanguinis*. The letter implemented the U.S. government policy for me to take residency in the U.S. so I wouldn't lose my citizenship at the age of twenty-one.

I was thrown into the crucible again: To stay in the country where I was born to live and serve, or to go where, except for my citizenship, I didn't belong. I recalled the thought that stuck in my mind since I was a kid: The gentle wind that blew my boat to the corners of the pond foreshadowed the journeys I would be taking, the places where I would be living and working after I had left my ancestral home in the Philippines.

Two years after, I crossed the Pacific Ocean to immigrate to the U.S., along with some members of my family. I decided to live in the United States in deference to the U.S. government policy.

In September 1975, I was accepted at St. Mark's Seminary in Southern California, to complete my priestly formation. Early on at St. Mark's, I thought of several options pertaining to how I could serve as a priest. By coincidence, the U.S. Military Chaplaincy did a national search for an Asian-American seminarian close to priesthood ordination. The recruiting team found me at St. Mark's and promised to offer me a chaplaincy assignment after my ordination. They gave me a choice for chaplaincy in the navy, army, air force, or the coast guard. It was an offer too good to ignore calling to mind that in my boyhood, I once dreamed of being a soldier. I turned the offer down. I was set on serving in the Archdiocese of Los Arboles. Since then, I built my dream around becoming and remaining a parish priest.

Three years later, in 1978, I completed my theological studies and priestly formation. I chose to be ordained for the Archdiocese of Los Arboles. On June 24 of that year, I was the first Filipino-born, a graduate from St. Mark's, who was ordained for the Archdiocese of Los Arboles. I felt blessed and empowered to blaze the trail for the other Filipino priests who would come after me to serve in the archdiocese. I took to heart the wisdom of the Spanish poem, *Caminante, no hay camino. Se hace el camino por andar* (Traveler, there is no road. The road is made as you travel on.)

Since my ordination, by providence, most of my parish assignments were near the coastline of Los Angeles County. In June 2003,

I celebrated my twenty-fifth Priesthood Ordination Anniversary. The theme I chose for that event was: "With You, O Lord, I Will Fish Other Seas." Angel's Gate Lighthouse was the inspiration and the center icon of the event's logo.

Angel's Gate Lighthouse, grounded on rock, built on a concrete base with steel columns and roof, stood atop the breakwater at the mouth of Long Beach Harbor. Its rotating green light flashed every fifteen seconds; its foghorn blasted every thirty, beaming out visibility as far as twenty miles, penetratingly reaching out and reverently touching people's lives and spirits. Since 1913, it had responded to distress calls from vessels lost at sea and guided them to the safely of the harbor. To this day, it still does in this place where information travels over cyberspace, and where digital communication defies space. Although not always visible due to bad weather, Angel's Gate has persevered in and has quietly done its work of guiding and bringing travelers, merchant sailors, and fishermen to safe harbor. Many times, in a stormy sea, under harsh conditions, it has saved lives.

I enjoyed gazing at Angel's Gate Lighthouse every time our sports fishing boat passed by it. Even for a fleeting moment of its view, it fascinated my imagination. I often imagined that many generations of our country's immigrants were welcomed and ushered in by it, long before airport towers did. It's a living reminder that its light, its welcoming energy traveling faster than sound did once convey to me, not in pronounced Tagalog, but in Morse code-like signals - *Mabuhay*, Welcome to America.

Only God knew! A year after, in July 2004, I was appointed pastor of St. Barnabas Church in Long Branch, a stone's throw away from Angel's Gate Lighthouse.

At my installation, I chose the theme "Journeying the Seas,

Anchored in Christ," in the tradition of St. Barnabas. On the day of my installation, I recalled to mind the lesson I learned from my childhood experience: To be a pastor is to accept the truth that humility is a sign of openness in receiving God's call to serve. To be a pastor is to believe that there is a higher power, in the form of a ripple or a light breeze, that directs my life and my ministry.

At my installation mass, as I stood in front of parish leaders and parishioners, I first turned toward the stained-glass window of St. Barnabas, off to the right side of the presider's chair. I spoke about the parish's patron saint, telling the congregation that I drew inspiration from St. Barnabas in whose honor our parish was named. As a young man, before his conversion, Barnabas offered his material possessions for the missionary works of the growing Christian community. He dedicated his life and shared his talents in the Lord's service. He left everything behind and spent the rest of his life preaching the Word of God. The maxim in Latin, *Deo optimo maximo* (to God, the best and the most), applied to St. Barnabas as my role model in generosity.

I was inspired further by Barnabas's courage amidst rejections and persecutions. He taught me to embrace Christ and to put into practice the message of the gospel in the face of hardships. Paul and Barnabas were met with rejection and persecution. In Antioch, some leaders in the community got jealous of Paul and Barnabas, countering their success with violent abuse and finally expelled them from their territory. The two did not lose heart. They courageously continued with their missionary journey. Paul died a violent death by the sword at the hands of the Romans sometime in AD 68. Barnabas also died a martyr during the persecution by Emperor Nero in the first century.

No man is an island, I said in my installation homily. No pastor can minister effectively all by himself. A parish without parishioners' participation is like a ship without a crew. The members of the mystical Body of Christ, endowed with a variety of personal and spiritual gifts, steer our parish forward, to the direction and to the destination the Lord has led us so far.

There will be myriad of trials and challenges ahead of us, I said further in my homily. I was preaching from a marble ambo. The palm of my hands lay comfortably flat on the gospel page as I continued to speak, stating that I believed that God who strengthened Barnabas amidst persecution by the Jews and the Romans would also strengthen us amidst the hard-to-comply demands of the archdiocese. Pointing to the large sculpted icons of the cross, anchor, and heart, symbols of the three theological virtues of faith, hope and charity, I suggested to the parishioners to think of ourselves as flukes of an anchor that clasp the ocean floor, giving stability to our parish through dedicated service.

Following in the footsteps of St. Barnabas, I promised the parishioners to be a sign of Christ's presence among them: to preside at weekend and weekday masses, to hear confessions, as per need, to counsel confused teenage girls against procuring abortions, and to anoint the sick and the dying, both those at home and in the hospital, among others.

3

The year 2005 was dismal. It was in the spring of that year that the district attorney of Los Angeles County served the Archdiocese of Los Arboles with 400 cases of clergy sexual abuse of minors.

One evening, as was my habit after a long day of work, that day having been spent interviewing high school students' readiness for the Sacrament of Confirmation, I worked out at the nearby LA Fitness. I set the treadmill at a moderate speed so I could watch the news on the big screen television on the wall. Not long thereafter, I was struck by the anchorwoman's report of the breaking news that a man hanged himself in the shower room. He was found dead. I turned the treadmill's speed down to a bare twenty miles per hour so I could concentrate on that breaking news. I reached for my towel, wiped off perspiration, and took a big gulp of water. According to the *Los Angeles Tribune*, the anchorwoman reported, the deceased was a priest from the Archdiocese of Los Arboles, who was being investigated by LAPD for sexual abuse of minors, but the archdiocese sent him to St. Luke's, an out-of-state institution for rehabilitation. The television screen focused on the dead body hanging from the shower, a rope tied tightly around his neck.

"Oh my God!" I exclaimed, shocked at the gruesome sight. It

was Father Teddy, the former pastor at St. Barnabas.

Moments later, my iPhone rang, registering Soller's caller ID. Soller told me that he happened to watch the news about Father Teddy. He wanted to see me at St. Barnabas first thing in the morning. I agreed.

The morning mass at which I presided had just ended. Many of those who attended it were on their way home or to their work. Some were still praying the Rosary inside the church. Soller arrived, anxious to talk to me. For privacy, I offered the sacristy as the place to talk. He agreed. In no time, he dropped a bombshell on me.

"The reason why you were appointed to take over the parish was that the archdiocese expected you to do a better job."

"I'm new in the neighborhood, barely getting acquainted with the people," I retorted. "I heard rumors about Father Teddy's activities while he was here.—"

"I don't want you to be nosy about the rumors and the rumor-mongers," Soller butted in. "It's better for you to play deaf."

"That's hard for me to do. I can't sweep dirt under the rug. What I hear or see around here becomes a part of me."

"By that, you are showing arrogance. Remember, you were ordained and sworn to obedience."

"True, but I weigh in on my decisions accordingly. I have the responsibility to tell the truth."

"I must remind you, whatever you heard about Father Teddy, I order you to observe the code of silence." That said, Soller stormed his way out of the sacristy to the parking lot, where he had parked in the space marked, *Clergy Only*.

As was my habit of going into the rectory after the morning mass, I went in through the back door, the shortcut between the rectory and the sacristy. The parish secretary met me in the corridor.

She had that look in her face telling me of something unusual that morning. "Someone's in your office," she warned me. "Martin. He insisted on seeing you. He said it's urgent."

When I went into my office, a man in his forties, his blue eyes downcast, his face a strong resemblance of a hush puppy, shook my hand and introduced himself as the regional coordinator of MAP, an acronym for Minors Abused by Priests. I closed my office door and invited Martin to have a seat. I took the other seat across from him in front of my desk. Then I put out my right hand, and with an open palm, I waved it in circular motions to signal him to speak.

"I was abused by our parish priest when I was in the seventh and eighth grade while I was attending Catholic school," Martin confided. "Since then, my life has been a mess. I have struggled to keep my faith. I have lost trust in those who have authority in the church. When the bishop moved the abusive priest to another parish, I found out later, that bastard priest abused even more people."

"So, what keeps you going?" I asked, pretending to be ignorant of the activities of MAP. At that time, newspapers, television news, and social media were on a feeding frenzy about clergy sexual abuses. On the national level, MAP has been publicized as the aggressive organization lobbying for monetary compensation for abused victims.

"Reaching out and working with victims and their families," Martin responded, his head up, his gaze meeting mine. "One of your parishioners contacted me about Father Teddy's case. We need to work together to bring this case to a closure. We need your help in the process."

"I-I-I don't know what to do. This comes as a surprise to me. Have you contacted the archbishop?"

"Several times, but he kept referring us to the regional bishop. Bishop . . ."

"Bishop Soller. What did he say?"

"He refuses to meet with us," Martin sounded exasperated. "Never mind the bishop. So, I decided to see you."

"Why?"

"You have the responsibility as a pastor," Martin stated sternly. "You have to protect the innocent lambs among your flock from the marauding wolves."

I was obliged to do so. "Do you have the name of the parishioner who contacted you?"

"The Wheelers, Barbara and Bob. Their teenage son's name is Jim."

That evening, I paid a visit to the Wheelers. Barbara answered the door. She ushered me to their living room. Her husband, Bob, was reclining on the couch watching the early-evening news. As soon as I took a seat, he turned off the television to give me the floor to speak.

"Martin from MAP shared with me some info about Father Teddy's relationship with Jim. I'm sorry."

Bob hesitated for a while, then called up enough courage to speak. "Barbara and I tried a few times to talk to Jim, but he refuses to talk to us."

Barbara spoke up next. "We trusted Father Teddy. He was very close to our Jimmy boy." She heaved a sigh. "Father Teddy awarded Jimmy the Best Altar Boy Award for three consecutive years in a row and took him to Disneyland several times and to movies other times. Father Teddy came with us on our family cruise to the Mexican Riviera. He and Jimmy were inseparable." Barbara folded her hands as if in prayer. "God forgive me, I gave Father Teddy a key to our house."

"Father Sal, can you help Barbara and me?" Bob's plea was like a prayer to St. Jude, the patron saint of the despairing. "We think that we are partly to be blamed for Father Teddy's suicide and Jimmy's isolation."

Barbara swiped a tear from her cheek. "When Jimmy heard the news, he threw away all the teddy bears Father Teddy gifted him with over the years. Jimmy locked himself in his room and refused to talk to anyone."

"I understand what Jim's going through and how deeply he's been hurting. I'm sorry. I wish I could help."

"Perhaps you can talk to him in private," Barbara suggested. "To convince him to testify at the court hearings."

"I can't promise, but I'll try."

As I stood up to leave, Barbara followed me to the door. She slipped Jim's mobile phone number into my shirt pocket.

A couple of days after, on my day off one spring morning, Jim and I played a one-on-one basketball game at the nearby Long Beach Recreational Park. We played for an hour. Then we agreed to call it a game. We stood briefly outside the painted markings on concrete, staring at the hoop.

"That was a clincher shot, Jim. You beat me," I conceded.

"At the buzzer," Jim remarked, his head tilted up, his eyes fixed on the hoop, his hands mimicking a Kobe Bryant shot. "I made it. St. Barnabas Boys Team clinched the championship that year."

I invited Jim to sit on a bench just outside of the basketball court. He sat down and put the ball down next to his feet, under the bench. I pulled out two bottles of Gatorade from my backpack. One for Jim and one for me. We both took big gulps of the energy drink.

"Jim, you blew me away when you responded to my text inviting you for a game of basketball. So good that you agreed to help me flex my muscles in that basketball game, even though I lost. What's my punishment?"

"Zip, zero. I dropped your chalice on the altar floor once while serving your mass. No score. You didn't drop me from the Altar Boy's List. No score."

"Jimmy boy," I mimicked his parents' calling him by that name, "I know how hard it is for you to be going through this difficult time ..." I said, not knowing how Jim would react. "And this I know is too much to ask of you . . . but can you testify at Father Teddy's court hearing?"

Jim stood up abruptly and kicked the ball so hard it landed on the other side of the basketball court. He hurled the Gatorade bottle down on the ground and stomped on it. I kept my mouth shut, patiently waiting for him to calm down. Then he sobbed. I waited more, taking a chance at the possibility that he might open up. Thank God, he did. He spoke through hiccups.

"I can't help you."

We didn't say a word to each other. We both gazed at the basketball hoop—a momentary impasse. Something similar to a crisis-negotiator crept up in me.

"You're a clincher, Jimmy boy," I said, flashing him three fingers, signifying three points. "You said you did it once. You sure can do it again. This time. When you are most needed."

Jim violently shook his head, covered his ears, and slumped back on the bench. It broke my heart, hearing my altar boy sob. I always remembered him attentively serving at my masses with such a winsome smile on his face.

I gently laid a hand on his shoulder. "Jimmy boy, please, we are a team. We are not playing one-on-one anymore. I'll call the DA to include you in his list of victim witnesses. And don't worry, I'll be there for you." I reached out for his hand. "I'll keep passing the ball to you." With my other hand, I flashed the three-finger sign once again.

"All right," Jim agreed. "I promise not to drop the ball." We high-fived. Then, we both walked away from the basketball court. I drove him home. His parents were anxiously waiting to talk to him. I knew that Jim was then ready to open up to his parents.

Two months had passed. The DA had served the Archdiocese of Los Arboles subpoenas to appear in Los Angeles Superior Court in the case of the James Wheeler Family vs. the Archbishop of Los Arboles, a corporation sole. Judge Holder was assigned as the presiding judge; Deputy District Attorney Jaime Contreras, the prosecutor; archdiocesan attorney Charles Langley, the defense attorney. Bishop Soller, who was subpoenaed, was to represent the archdiocese. The hearing was scheduled on Friday of that last week of the month. The Wheelers, who had received their summons, invited me as their moral support. I agreed.

I rode with the Wheelers on the way to the hearing. When we were entering the main door of the courthouse, our attention was caught by a boisterous group of protesters. A group of approximately fifty people partly blocked the entrance. Some of them were holding up antichurch protest placards, and one of them had a loudspeaker.

From the distance, I heard the voice of the man holding the loudspeaker, chanting, "Priests abusers!" The rest of the protestors chanted in turn, "Yes, you are!" Then again, the man with loudspeaker boomed with, "Bishops abusers," to which the protestors amplified it with their own, "Yes, you are!" At that, because of the tone of his voice, I recognized that the one on the loudspeaker was Martin; the protestors, MAP members.

The Wheelers and I passed through the main door on the way to the courtroom. But we stopped and turned around to find out why the voices of the protesters rose to a crescendo. The protestors, huddled at the main door, blocking the entrance, clashed with a team of courthouse security. I excused myself from the Wheelers and ran to see what the commotion was. I found out that the protestors were blocking Soller and the archdiocesan attorney from entering through the main door. The sight of protestors and security officers pushing and shoving one another was disconcerting. The protestors outnumbered the security officers.

One of the security officers called LAPD. In no time, the call was answered with half a dozen black-and-white police cars with flashing lights arriving at the scene. The police officers in riot gear swarmed the site with their own loudspeakers, ordering the protestors to let Soller and the attorney to go through the main door so they could make it to the court hearing.

The protestors gave in. But many of them entered the courthouse. I could only guess that since they didn't take with them the loudspeaker and the placards inside the courthouse, they intended to observe silence while the court was in session.

Inside the chamber, Afro American Judge Holder, in his sixties, sat confidently on the presiding chair. He announced, "This court is now open to resume the hearings on the Wheeler case. Let me start with the testimony from the next witness, James Wheeler."

"Your Honor, the record says that James Wheeler is a minor," Langley, the defense attorney, objected. "I move that he should not take the stand." Langley was a former Los Angeles Superior Court DA. He was a tall, trim Irishman, looking like an FBI officer at a swearing-in ceremony. Once before that hearing, Langley set up a meeting with me to try to persuade me not to testify against the archdiocese. He advised that I should be on the side of the archdiocese, just like in his case. He told me that at his retirement from the county's superior court, and coincidentally, at the outbreak of the sexual abuse by priests' scandal on the national level, he decided, out of the goodness of his heart, to volunteer to work for the Archdiocese of Los Arboles.

"I move to disagree with the defense, Your Honor," Contreras, the deputy DA, countered. Contreras was a bearded man, a Cervantes look-alike. "I hereby invoke the court to call on Father Sal Galvez, James's pastor, to act as his adult moral support."

"Motion granted," Judge Holder said. He then signaled to Contreras to call Jim and me up to the podium. Contreras caressed the end of his beard, then nodded to Jim and me.

Jim and I stood up and walked up to the stand. I escorted Jim to stand in front of the podium, my hand soft on his shoulder. Jim coughed, almost choking. He cleared his throat. Then he spoke up, his voice sounding in an intermittent high-low tone.

"Many times, Father Teddy took me to his room in the rectory. With the door locked, he tackled me down to his bed and sexually abused me. I resisted, but he overpowered me. At times, when I got out of his grip, he promised me that he wouldn't do it again. But it happened again—many more times. Since then, my life's a garbage. Up to now."

I heard people inside the chamber emit a round of pained gasps. Barbara Wheeler sobbed. Bob reached out for his wife's hand, squeezing it tightly. Jim took a step back from the mic, sobbing. I believed he didn't want to speak anymore. I squeezed his shoulder to encourage him to talk as I whispered in his ears, "Jimmy boy, we're a team, remember?" Jim stepped up to the mic again to speak.

"That day when Bishop Soller came to say mass in our parish, I served at his mass. After the mass, I told him about what Father Teddy had been doing to me. Bishop Soller got mad at me. He told me that I lied. As punishment, he told me that he would order Father Teddy to take me off the serving list."

I heard another round of pained gasps. Martin and MAP members stood up and pointed a finger at Bishop Soller. Soller remained seated, the defense attorney by his side. Soller clutched his pectoral cross, keeping his head down. The defense attorney stood up to speak. "Your Honor, I move for the protection of Bishop Soller's name. I invoke the separation of the church and state privilege."

"Declined," Judge Holder said. "The privilege does not apply to criminal cases such as what we have here. This court does not condone criminal acts against minors." That said, the judge's gavel hit the wood surface with a sound that echoed throughout the entire courtroom. "The violating institutions will have to pay compensation to the victims."

In the summer of that year, the DA served the Archdiocese of Los Arboles with yet another round of subpoenas to appear in Los Angeles Superior Court. I was also served because I was then pastor of St. Barnabas parish. The court hearing was scheduled on Friday of that last week in August. Judge Holder, Jaime Contreras, and Charles Langley remained in their official roles. Bishop Soller showed up, still under court subpoena. Martin and about a dozen others showed up as MAP reps.

Inside the Los Angeles County Superior Courtroom, Judge Holder called out, "This court is now open to resume the hearings on the case, The People of Los Angeles County vs. the Archbishop of Los Arboles, a corporation sole. I now call the next witness, Father Sal Galvez."

Jaime Contreras, the deputy district attorney, motioned to me to take the witness stand. I stood up and walked up to the mic. I raised my right hand and swore to tell the truth as per court protocol. Judge Holder looked over the top page of the stack of documents on his desk and then looked up at me.

"The record shows that you replaced Father Teddy at St. Barnabas. Is that right?"

"Yes, Your Honor."

"The deputy DA said you volunteered to speak against the archdiocese. Why is that?"

"Your Honor, the Archdiocese of Los Arboles has been silent about clergy sexual abuses of minors. My conscience obliges me to do something about it."

Charles Langley, the archdiocesan defense attorney, motioned to speak. The judge gave him the floor. "Your Honor, Father Sal can't be a fair witness because he is not an abuse victim himself. I move that he shouldn't give a testimony."

"Declined."

Contreras, the deputy DA, asked to speak too. Judge Holder gave him the floor. He addressed the judge. "Some of my clients had witnessed sexual abuse in their teenage years. I move that Father Sal speak . . . speak on their behalf."

"Granted."

Cold perspiration ran down my face. I moved closer to the mic and cleared my throat. My voice sounded falsetto. "My best friend was an abused victim . . . at the hands of a priest, our former teacher, when my friend and I were in high school seminary in the Philippines. My friend confided to me that the priest offered him high grades for sexual favors. When he refused, the priest threatened him with expulsion from our class. After their 'rendezvous,' as the abusing priest used to call it, he offered money to my friend to buy books and snacks. The abuser ordered my friend not to tell anyone about it. But instead, my friend told his secret to me."

An uproar was heard among the people inside the courtroom. The members of MAP who came to witness the hearing turned to

Soller with a disdainful look. He hung his head and buried his face in his hands.

An irreverent silence filled the courtroom.

At that moment, my thoughts sank to a deep past. A repressed memory surged up from the dark recesses of my mind: *Later that year, after the abuse revelation by my friend, another sad incident happened. Another friend of mine and I were in the seminary infirmary, down with the flu. The infirmarian, a professed religious brother, as was his duty, brought food and medicine to those of us confined in the infirmary. But something else happened. The infirmarian sat on my friend's bed and groped him. My friend was too sick to fight him off. I wanted to stop it, but I was scared and too sick to do anything. I just looked away, feeling paralyzed—powerless.* I had been a silent witness.

The uproar in the courtroom was still loud when my mind drifted back to the moment. It was then I realized that deep inside me, the silence of grief and shame, one that I never gave a voice to for years since 1964, at last, by my public testimony in court, erupted to the loudness of a protest chant.

4

In February 2011, almost three years before my dismissal from St. Barnabas, I was called for a meeting in Soller's office. When I entered the meeting room, Soller was already seated. He motioned me to sit on the chair to his side. Laid out on the desk in front of me was a stack of files that, in my mind, was deliberately set to intimidate me.

"*Suwerte ka at wala pa ako sa region ng San Pio habang nasa Holy Trinity ka*," Soller said in Tagalog. The tone of his voice was sarcastic, telling me how lucky I was that he was not around when I was the pastor at Holy Trinity from 1992–2004. Underneath his words were intimidation and veiled threats.

He held a folder which he claimed contained the report from the recent parish audit, which he ordered and was conducted by Mr. Hilt Switchseyer from October to December 2010. Switchseyer, an accountant from some obscure financial company in Southern California, was recently hired by the Archdiocese of Los Arboles' Finance Department. I didn't know about his credentials. I didn't care. But I imagined that by his name, sounding like "glib talker," he probably touched the right button and found his way in to the Finance Department.

When I leaned over to take a look at the open folder on top of the stack, Soller pulled it back, making sure that I didn't get even a passing glimpse of the papers.

"How did the report get to your hand?" I asked Soller, wondering why Switchseyer's audit report was already in his possession. "As agreed in our initial audit meeting, Switchseyer promised me to review the audit report first before anybody else sees it. He broke his promise of confidentiality."

"I asked for it," Soller replied.

"Why? What was your intent?" I asked. To avoid seeing Soller's face turn blackish-red, I shifted my attention to the glass window through which my gaze momentarily perched on the ripe lemons from the tree outside Soller's office.

"This report serves as proof of your ineptness as a pastor."

I shifted my gaze back to Soller, seeing in him a resemblance to a lemon that smells sweet only on the outside. "Is financial issue the sole criterion for assessing pastors?"

"For me, yes," he said. "It might have made a difference if St. Barnabas had a functional Finance Council."

"We do, since 2004, when I started as pastor," I asserted. "And way before it."

"How come it is not reflected in the audit report?"

I told Soller that three months prior, at the end of the audit sessions, Switchseyer assured me that most audit materials were pretty much in place. That before Switchseyer requested the minutes of the Parish Finance Council meetings, I asked him to put his request in writing either by formal letter or email. He promised to email me as soon as he got back to his office. But I never received either an electronic or a hard copy from him. The binder that contained the minutes of the Finance Council meetings, the one that Switchseyer required to be stored in the parish safe, had long been kept there.

Furthermore, as per requirement by the Finance Department, I had been complying by sending minutes of the Parish Finance Council meetings to our dean every three months.

"Parishioners are calling the Regional Office, complaining about you," Soller said after he placed the folder that he was holding on top of the other ones on his desk.

"Who are they?" I asked, pointing at the stack of files, guessing that the list of those who complained about me was in one of them. "I need to know about their complaints so I can take the time to address the issues and work diligently to resolve conflicts or to offer guidance."

There was a stony look on Soller's face. Neither did he identify the persons, nor the nature of their complaints.

The day after, I initiated a committee, the Strategy for a Stronger Parish. It was composed of our parish council president, finance council chair, my associate pastor, and I. The goal of the committee was to develop a financial plan and set of actions to balance the budget. The committee met once a month.

A month later, I sent a report to Soller, documenting the items taken up at the meetings and our plan to implement them. Soller did not acknowledge nor respond to my letter. His silence spoke volumes. In his silence, I felt being choked by him. His hands, heavy with authority, were pressed firmly on my throat. I felt left out and alone in the dark, suffocating.

Soller's silence spelled out for me the culture of clericalism. I read him as a bishop cloaked and imprisoned in his self-created world, morosely detaching himself from someone below his rank. Looking at this disintegrating personality of a church representative made me believe that clericalism was a contagious disease, one that corresponds to the lyrics of Paul Simon's song, "Silence like a cancer grows."

As contagious and cancerous the silence of Soller was, it did contaminate his administrative assistant, Rob Schaeffer. Schaeffer was an ordained permanent deacon serving in the San Pio Region. I know that in early Christianity, deacons were ordained for works of charity. But I imagined that Schaeffer had the impression that by serving under Soller, he was doing sort of charitable works when he wrote to me, "*I have been directed to monitor and follow up on what the Regional Office has received over the past five years. There are a number of parishioners who have alleged they don't feel that they are listened to, so they seek other archdiocesan representatives to voice their concerns.*"

At that, I wondered about the correlative behavior of the bishop and his administrative assistant. I wondered further why these complaints were kept in the Regional Office and not in the Archdiocesan Catholic Center. Something's boiling up. Something's cooked up—a collusion of clericalism in the Regional Office—a stonewalling act taking center stage.

So I responded to Schaeffer's letter. I wrote, "*Concerning parishioners' complaints, I do observe professional, canonical, and pastoral practices in handling them. The Archdiocesan Department of Human Resources obliges that those against whom complaints had been lodged be informed. Complaints or issues formally brought to my attention have been dealt with and resolved. I cannot be held accountable for complaints over the last five years that have not been brought up to my attention. I have the right to know what goes into my files.*"

I have not heard from Schaeffer since, except for his explanation that he was Soller's delegate, a title whose practices, I observed, revealed him as the bishop's hatchet man. Soller's collaborators easily formed a clericalism groundswell of sorts as it spilled out wider to the archdiocesan financial staff.

Two months after my meeting with Soller, Wally Stinger, the

archdiocesan chief financial officer, called me for a meeting to talk about the audit that was conducted by Switchseyer. The meeting took place at the Archdiocesan Catholic Center, where the offices of those who reported to Archbishop Fernandez were located. Also, present were Schaeffer representing Soller, and Switchseyer, the auditor hired by Stinger. They all wore coat and tie, the dress code for formal meetings. I came dressed in black, but I did not put my clerical collar on.

At the meeting, Schaeffer gave me the impression that the notes he took were going straight to Soller. Switchseyer, absentmindedly, kept tapping on his black leather portfolio except during moments he had to hand a report to Stinger. Like a snake in the grass, Switchseyer coiled on top of his audit reports, awaiting an opportune time to spurt venom at me.

"Your parish owes a large amount of money to the archdiocese. It's more than a million dollars," Stinger said, looking over the document the auditor handed him. "Why is the parish not able to pay its dues?" The tone of his voice was a stinger, indeed, just as his name is, as a matter of fact.

"We are paying eight thousand dollars a month," I replied. "But due to the current economy adversely affecting our parish as evidenced by the drop in the collection, our parish is not able to pay the full amount we owe the archdiocese."

"Archbishop Fernandez and Bishop Soller require all parishes to settle their dues. It's the archdiocesan priority," Stinger declared, breathing fire through his thick mustache.

"I am working conscientiously with the Parish Finance Council members toward a balanced budget. I meet with them every other month, and lately, every month."

"You just meet," Stinger said, the tone of his voice loaded with sarcasm, one that I interpreted to mean that our parish leaders and I were not doing enough.

"We are doing more than you thought we do," I said assertively. "I initiated and implemented staff cuts and salary freezes without sacrificing pastoral and educational programs. Yet, the rising cost of living and operations could not bridge the gap between expenses and incomes. The gap widened over the years."

I peeked through the half-open door separating Stinger's office, where we were having the meeting to the workroom of his staff of secretaries and accountants working on computers, making copies of reports, and preparing checks for Stinger's signature. I wondered why Stinger kept so many staff while I cut mine to a skeletal staffing.

"I'll call a meeting with you, the parish bookkeeper, and the chair of the Parish Finance Council," Stinger offered. "We have to assure the archbishop that we are serious about financial accountability." Detecting a smirk on his face, I knew early on that he was not sincere.

Stinger never called us for a meeting. His silence, operating under a dark cloud of his collusion with Soller, enveloped and poisoned many in his department. It was ironic that he who spoke of transparency at meetings, exhibited opposite behavior.

A few months later, I received a letter from Bishop Soller demanding that I send him a report that our parish leaders and I had balanced the budget. In response to Soller's demand for a balanced budget, our Parish Finance Council made a recommendation to sell the two houses owned by the parish. The market value of those properties totaled to at least $600,000. Taking into consideration the Parish Finance Council's recommendation, I wrote a letter to Soller seeking his approval for the sale of the real estate properties. Archdiocesan policy required the permission of the regional bishop before Stinger could approve it.

Soller never acknowledged nor responded to my letter.

Likewise, in response to Soller's demand for a balanced parish budget, in October 2013, I wrote a letter to Stinger informing him of the Parish Finance Council's plan to request that the thirty-five thousand dollars loaned by our parish to the archdiocese, a loan that was contracted with Archbishop O' Malley's initiative to help pay out money settlement with the victims of the clergy sexual abuse of minors, was not paid by the archdiocese. The loan would have been paid to our parish in 2012, and be credited to St. Barnabas parish as a way of reducing our debt to the archdiocese. Furthermore, I told Stinger that our Parish Finance Council requested that the monthly interest from the Investment Pool, an investment of $230,000 deposited in the archdiocese, be arranged in such a way that monthly interests be paid out to the archdiocese as another way to reduce our debt.

Nothing was heard from Stinger. The conspiracy of sacred silence had contaminated the bloodstream of the Finance Department.

A month later, Bishop Soller called me, telling me that he wanted to meet with the members of the Parish Finance Council and me. Raul, a middle-aged fishing buddy of mine and chair of St. Barnabas Parish Finance Council, prepared the agenda. The meeting took place in St. Barnabas parish hall. At the meeting, when I informed Soller that Raul and I were to present the plan to pay parish debt, he said *no* to it in a condescending way. Instead, he spoke extensively about the debt, and he made sure that the Finance Council members and I took the blame for it.

"It's your parish," Soller said in a nonchalant tone of voice, referring to the parish debt.

"How do we know that the Archdiocese has an accurate

accounting of our parish debt?" Raul asked.

"It's your responsibility," Soller responded. "I'm assigning you to call the Finance Department."

The day after the meeting, Raul called Switchseyer about the specifics of the debt. Switchseyer could not supply the entire record. He said that there was a change in the computer system, and that the missing records were stored somewhere else.

Ironically, why should Soller be hard on us, when he should be hard on the archdiocese which had been in the red for years? In July 2007, the archdiocese agreed on a global settlement of four hundred milion dollars to pay for the four hundred civil cases involving clergy accused of sexual abuse of minors. The debt balance of the archdiocese was 200 million dollars. Rather than scapegoat the parish for his poor leadership, both in the archdiocese and San Pio Region, Soller should have stood up to the archdiocese and challenged its *modus operandi* of scapegoating. What was he afraid of? Or was he simply content on being a cowardly clerical vassal, one who could not stand up to speak for me after he had slashed my vocal cords?

June 25, 2011, the day I celebrated my thirty-fourth ordination anniversary, was also the day of yet another meeting with Soller. Cognizant of the importance of being prepared, I collected and studied relevant parish financial documents, placed them in a folder, and brought them to the meeting. Deacon Schaeffer, Switchseyer, Raul, and I participated in that meeting.

At the meeting, I expressed my thanks to Soller on behalf of the Pastoral Council and the Finance Council for calling us to work together on the finances of the parish. Switchseyer acknowledged that St. Barnabas paid eight thousand dollars a month to the archdiocese. He reported further that Pedro Gutierrez, the parish custodian, and his family, who were renting one of the two parish houses, are the subjects of complaints by some parishioners. In that particular section of his report, Switchseyer commented, "The pastor, on his own, made the arrangement without the knowledge of the Finance Department. And as a consequence, such action by the pastor had opened up to parishioners' complaints." Switchseyer, another hatchet man of Soller's, by manipulating his audit report to fit Soller's agenda, had been sucked in to the clerical culture in the Archdiocese of Los Arboles.

"I'm taking this personally," I butted in. Taking a page from the folder, I flashed the "Contract of Lease" page before Switchseyer's eyes. "Here, can't you see? The archdiocesan director of the Real Estate Department signed it." I eyed Switchseyer first, then Schaeffer with a pointed question. "Don't you guys in the same damn department ever communicate?"

"I disagree with the accountant's report," Raul spoke up. "We, as parish leaders, had not heard of any complaints against the Gutierrez family. I know in my heart that Pedro and his family are deeply religious, hardworking, and of good moral character."

"And I question the audit's objectivity," I added.

Soller, in his usual condescending way, and in spite of his letter of invitation stating it was a "dialogue meeting," cut me off by blurting out, "No need for more proof. The audit is conclusive."

Raul told Soller off. "Your insensitivity toward Pedro and his family is causing an erosion of trust and respect among parish leaders. If you were a respectable church authority, would you first investigate for yourself, then make *your* decision based on *your* own findings, rather than rely solely on an auditor's biased report?" He took a deep breath. Then he breathed out, "And you, Bishop, should have taken into account our pastor's point of view. Incorporate yours with his. Your joint decision makes for genuine and excellent leadership practice." Raul violently shook his head. "What's ironic is that your voice sounds official, but your action is not that respectable. You have become your own worst enemy."

Soller spoke up, the palms of his hands raised in a stop-talking gesture, but his eyes glared at me. "I give you one year . . . one year to straighten out the parish finances," he barked at me, ". . . including the full implementation of the audit recommendation." He dropped his hands, turned to Raul, and ordered him, "See to it that these are complied with." He turned to me again, this time with an obliging look, "Evaluate whether you should still be at St. Barnabas."

Should Soller rather be asking himself whether he should be at the place where he was, and in the office he was occupying? Priests and laity in the archdiocese were in the dark about why he was transferred to San Pio Region. A few years before his transfer, he worked as director of Propagation of Faith in the Archdiocesan Catholic Center. The silence surrounding his change of assignment, though, was deafening because the people of God cannot stop asking questions about the move. The secrecy surrounding his appointment might have been construed as a riddle and opened the situation to further mistrust of church leadership.

What Pope Paul VI said years back made sense to me. That the church had to look with penetrating eyes within herself and ponder the mystery of her own being. That vivid and lively self-awareness inevitably led to a comparison between the ideal image of the church as Christ had envisaged and had loved her, and the actual image which the church had presented to the world today. Likewise, I dare say, Soller needed to examine himself as every church leader should. He needed to look into himself deeply and to have the humility to accept his flaws and resolve to do better for the sake of the church that he claimed he represented.

5

On March 2013, I celebrated my sixty-second birthday. That evening, my eyes pinned on the television screen, I saw a dark gray and white seagull perched on the chimney atop the roof of the Sistine Chapel. Down below, inside the chapel, 115 cardinal-electors from around the world were on their final balloting to elect the new pope. The magnified image of the seagull seen by millions of television viewers and social media users from giant video screens along the Bernini colonnade entertained the tens of thousands of people who gathered at St. Peter's Square in Rome to welcome the new pope. The seagull sat comfortably, at times pecking around the iron cap of the chimney. Shortly past 7:00 p.m., the seagull flew away.

At 7:05 p.m., Rome time, a puff of gray smoke, followed by a large puff of white billowed out of the chimney to the cheers of the gathered faithful on-site. Their cheers of *"Viva il Papa"* (Long Live the Pope) filled the air, which, in my imagination, drowned the noises of Rome's night life. The festive spirit of the cheerers lit up the square, even though night had already fallen.

As more white smoke billowed out, puffs wafted through the air, drifting over the statues of St. Peter, of the other disciples, and of the saints along the colonnade and above the crowd. On television, I heard the bells of St. Peter's Basilica peal in jubilation. I imagined those of the neighboring churches in Rome did too. In an instant, two words in Latin, *Habemus Papam* (We have a pope), flashed on my television screen. I imagined it did too on millions of social media screens throughout the world. Upon hearing the news, I imagined that many Catholics all over the world, their local church bells ringing to announce the much-anticipated good news, blessed themselves and prayed in gratitude for the new pope.

An hour after the white smoke signaled the election of the new pope, the senior cardinal spoke from the balcony above the main entrance of St. Peter's Basilica, "I announce to you with great joy. We have a pope—His Most Eminent and Revered Lord, Jorge Cardinal Bergoglio, who has chosen for himself the name, Francis." Pope Francis, who came from Argentina, became the next successor of Peter, the fisherman, and the head of the Roman Catholic Church whose membership included 1.2 billion Catholics.

Dressed in a plain wool, white cassock, white silk sash, and white skullcap, the new pope addressed the jubilant crowd from the balcony. "And now, let us begin this new journey, a journey of brotherhood in love, of mutual trust." Cheers from the jubilant crowd at St. Peter's Square rose to a deafening decibel. "Let us pray for one another," Pope Francis continued with his exhortation. "Let us pray for the whole world that there might be a great sense of brotherhood. My hope is that this journey of the church that we begin today may be fruitful for the evangelization of this beautiful city."

His words resonated with me because I too felt the invitation to walk on a new path. "Yes," I shouted over the television screen, "I'm with you. I will always remember you being my best birthday gift ever."

So, why was the presence of the seagull atop the chimney of the Sistine Chapel a meaningful sight to me?

Seagulls are fishermen's best friends. They are their eyes in the sky. Fishermen and birds fish together. When fishermen see the birds diving on a school of bait fish, fun-fishing begins. In spite of the high-tech "fish finders" that skippers use to spot schools of fish in the water, to me, there are no better fish finders than seagulls in the sky. Often seen around fishing boats, this flock of noisy, ravenous birds thrives on the art of fishing. I remember one day when our fishing boat was on the way back to the dock after a day of fishing, the deckhand was filleting fish, sliced open its belly up to extract entrails, carved the skin off its flesh, and tossed the skeleton with the head on into the air. I saw a seagull, poised in midair, dive with precision and perfect timing for it. Its catch was securely clipped between its sharp yellow beaks. At that sight, I conjured that fishermen learn a lot from seagulls in the way they fish and secure their catch.

Could that seagull be Pope Francis's "eye in the sky"?

"Yes" was my answer to my own question because seagulls and popes work together as fishermen, figuratively, fishers of men, fishers of peoples. As head and a team leader, Pope Francis charted a new course for the Catholic Church. And by doing so, I believed he whisked me out of the bureaucratic whirlpool the Archdiocese of Los Arboles threw me in.

Two months after his election, Pope Francis wrote his first pastoral letter, *Lumen Fidei* (Light of Faith). The pastoral letter reminded me that Christ is the true light. In it, Pope Francis exhorted me, his modern-day disciple, to be a bearer of this light to the ends of the earth. He encouraged me to speak publicly about my faith in the living God and of my personal friendship with Christ so that a few more people, especially those who live in darkness, may turn to the light of faith.

Weeks thereafter, Pope Francis addressed the cardinals, bishops, and priests working in the Vatican, pointing out to them the "fifteen ailments of the Vatican bureaucracy," one of which was clericalism—the ailment present among cardinals, bishops, and priests who use their careers to grab power and wealth, and of living hypocritical, double lives. "The terrorism of gossip," the pope further said, "can kill the reputation of our colleagues and brothers in cold blood. Cliques can enslave their members and become a cancer that threatens the harmony of the body and eventually kill it off by friendly fire." At the end of his address, Pope Francis asked the Vatican clergy to pray that the "wounds of the sins that each one of us carries are healed."

"How true, how true," I said to myself. Clericalism in the Vatican, like cancer, had contaminated the Archdiocese of Los Arboles and threatened to kill my priestly identity. Deeply wounded and abused by my superiors and their staff, denied the due canonical process, my human dignity tarnished, I refuse to be scapegoated and be sacrificed to the false god of clericalism. I decided to be an antidote to the violence inflicted on me by Soller and his clericalized lay staff, who had been acting as badly as their boss.

With the super typhoon Yolanda, internationally named Haiyan, that hit the Philippines on November 8, 2013, fresh in his mind, Pope Francis announced from the Vatican that he planned to visit the Philippines. At that very moment, he invited those gathered at St. Peter's Square to pray especially for the beloved people of the Philippines gravely affected by the recent typhoon.

6

The day after my removal from St. Barnabas, I called Archbishop Fernandez to request an emergency meeting with him. The archbishop, hearing both confusion and desperation in my voice, gladly accepted my request.

The meeting took place in his office at the Archdiocesan Catholic Center. The archbishop wore the traditional Roman Catholic archbishop attire: black wool cassock with purple silk sash, piping, and skullcap. On his desk lay a stack of prayer cards. Behind his chair hung a large crucifix, flanked by a framed photo of Our Lady of Guadalupe, a reproduction of the original displayed for public veneration at the Metropolitan Cathedral in Mexico City.

I reverently gazed at the image of Our Lady of Guadalupe. I felt at ease in her spiritual presence. I felt the same comfort I used to feel being in the church named in honor of Our Lady of Guadalupe, where I was baptized and made my first communion. It was there that I first heard of the story of the Virgin Mother (later named by the Spanish missionaries "Our Lady of Guadalupe"), who first appeared to the Indian peasant, Juan Diego, on December 1531 on the hills of Tepeyac near Mexico City. The Virgin of Guadalupe's message, originally said to Juan Diego, echoed in my ears: "*I am your merciful Mother, the Mother of all who live in this land, of all mankind, of all who love me, of those who have confidence in me. Here, I will hear their weeping and their sorrows. I will remedy and alleviate their sufferings, necessities, and misfortune."*

The archbishop motioned to me to take a seat across from his desk. I waited for him to take his seat. With the high backrest and elevated armrest, the archbishop looked sunken on his black leather chair. Notwithstanding, I could see his roundish face, his thick glasses telescoping his dark, brownish eyes.

"*Que hay?*" he said as a greeting, which I thought was his way of finding out if I spoke Spanish, and at the same time, to give me the floor to speak.

"*Gracias, su excelencia,*" was my reverential opening line. I quickly moved from courtesy to business. "Our parish has dutifully implemented your five pastoral priorities, one of which is to promote vocation to the priesthood and the religious life."

"Good to hear it," the archbishop commented. "The padre in the village in Mexico, where my family used to live, encouraged me to be a priest."

In a low tone, I sadly confided to the archbishop that our parish had been experiencing financial hardship. The economic recession that had affected millions of Americans in the mid-2000s did not spare St. Barnabas parish. Many parishioners had lost their jobs due to the economic downturn. Our parish, then considered upwardly mobile Pacifica, a district within the parish and a remainder of the oil boom industry in nearby Seaview Hill, had changed.

I told the archbishop that the change in demographics was another factor. St. Barnabas used to have white, upper- and middle-class parishioners. Within the last four years, I observed that the parish turned from upper-middle class to middle and lower-middle class. Over the last eight years or so, and especially over the last five, a large number of lower-middle class and poor people of various ethnic groups had made St. Barnabas their spiritual home. The pioneers of the parish were gradually dying off. Their children had relocated to other cities.

"What did you do to address the financial shortfall and to keep the parish financially sustainable?" the archbishop asked.

"It was so hard for our parish to make all ends meet," I sighed. I then explained to him that because of the priests' sexual abuse scandals, offertory and charitable giving to the Catholic Church in the USA dropped by 21 percent. The above-mentioned factors, plus increased archdiocesan assessments, rising operation, and insurance contributed to the reality that the parish incomes didn't match expenses. Of the 800 registered families, only 20 percent gave their donations on a weekly basis. Due to a lack of adequate education and motivational practices, the national average of Catholic giving was only 1–2 percent. This too was the situation at St. Barnabas.

With the vision of a holy and healthy parish which was initiated the previous year, I told the archbishop, I worked closely with Parish Finance and Pastoral Councils with two goals in mind: to pay the monthly bill of sixteen thousand dollars and to reduce the outstanding parish debt to the archdiocese. I paused to call up enough courage to say, "I tried my best to live up to the challenges."

I then shared with the archbishop detailed information about the "Called in Baptism, United in the Eucharist Parish Stewardship" program, which I initiated to encourage parishioners to be generous with their time, talent, and treasure. The goal of the program was to develop a parish-based, year-round stewardship program focusing on increased offertory incomes with the goal of a 5 percent increase in Sunday offertory collections. I invited parishioners to stewardship seminars in the parish hall. I wrote a series of articles about how to help increase church donations.

I saw a faint smile on the archbishop's face. I wasn't sure, though, if he was just trying to be polite, didn't want to be bothered, or that I should not have asked for that meeting in the first place.

The urgency of the subject I needed to inform the archbishop about didn't allow me to hold back. I revealed to him the depressing situation involving some of the families whose children were victims of clergy abuse: Some thirty cases of sexual abuse of minors at the hand of Father Teddy occurred at St. Barnabas and nearby parishes during the late '90s. Most of the victims were members of the pioneering families.

Up to this moment, I realized that the archbishop was trying to weigh in on the content of my narrative. He shifted his position with a posture that looked like sitting at the edge of his chair. A line of perspiration formed in his already wrinkled forehead. He adjusted his skullcap and turned his episcopal ring.

"What have you done to ensure that abuses of this kind did not happen on your watch?" he asked.

"Safeguarding and protecting future abuse of children and minors were my top priorities," I replied.

I did cooperate with city and federal law enforcement agents on the class-action lawsuits against the archdiocese. I answered their questions about what I knew of the accused priest and of what happened, though I had little to say because I was not there at the time. Since some victims alleged that abuses happened in the sacristy, choir area, priests' quarters, and in the youth center, I showed the referred-to places to the investigators. Based on their recommendations, I made renovations of those places to ensure that no abuses happened there again. Every year, I filed a report of full compliance in the safeguarding and protection of minors and sent it to the archdiocese.

Months before my meeting with the archbishop, in my meetings with parish leaders, I dared to tell them that those in church leadership, both on the local and national levels, denied and stonewalled the clergy abuses of minors. It was not until in the early 2000s that most of the victims and their families reported the cases to law enforcement authorities.

At masses, after informing parishioners about the financial situation, I invited them to participate in the increased offertory income. I called upon the entire parish community to share its gifts at the service of the various ministries. In the tradition of St. Barnabas, I encouraged the parishioners to lay their gifts at the feet of the apostles for the glory of God and service to God's people. As part of my stewardship commitment, I donated 5 percent of my salary to the parish fund. I participated in the archdiocesan-sponsored workshops on parish finances, administration, and personnel, including those given at catholic universities in Southern California . I enrolled in the "Good Leaders, Good Shepherds," Catholic Institute leadership program for priests. The institute focused on learning and practice according to the examples of Jesus, the Good Shepherd—the model by which bishops and priests carry out their pastoral ministry. I completed the course a year and a half after that. Archbishop Fernandez, who was present at our graduation ceremony, handed out the certificates to our class with his congratulatory words.

Toward the end of the meeting, the archbishop said, "Bishop Soller convinced me that keeping you at St. Barnabas will hurt the archdiocese more."

"Why?" I asked as if being stun-gunned by his episcopal ring finger pointed at me.

"Bishop Soller and I agree that you had been negligent in the administration of parish finances. So, it's time to bring in new blood, a new pastor, who can make a difference."

The archbishop stood up to pick up a copy of the prayer card from the stack lying on his desk. The front side of the card was printed with the image of Our Lady of Guadalupe; on the other side, with a prayer for vocation to the priesthood and religious life. I looked at it reverently, making a sign of the cross.

"I regret that I can't rescind our decision over your removal," the archbishop said as he extended his arm to hand me the card.

I remained seated, stunned.

A few seconds passed. I realized the archbishop's arm was still extended, so I took the card.

"May I give this to my mother?" I asked. "She has a strong devotion to Our Lady of Guadalupe."

"As you wish," the archbishop replied.

In spite of how I felt but out of respect for my superior, I knelt before him asking for his blessing, which he gave me.

I left after I reverenced his ring.

7

Actually, I didn't have five days to move out. In three out of those five days, I traveled to a retreat house in Northern California to participate in the Catholic School Pastors' Conference from March 28–30, 2014. It was scheduled months earlier. I went there as per Soller's directive.

While in the retreat house's chapel, in front of the Blessed Sacrament, I started writing my parting homily to be delivered at St. Barnabas that coming weekend.

Dear Brothers and Sisters in Christ, I wrote, *you might be wondering why for the first time in my ten years and three months of service to you as your pastor here at St. Barnabas, I stand and speak from the presider's chair and not from the ambo. You might be thinking: Something's going on, something out of the ordinary. Yes, I have a surprise announcement to make. But before I do that, allow me to reflect with you on the message of today's Gospel (Mt. 21:28–32).*

The gospel was about a father who had two sons. The father told his first son to work in the vineyard. The son agreed but did not go. Then the father spoke to his second son, asking him to work in the same vineyard. The second son was unwilling at first, but in the end, went. I identified myself with the second son. I was hesitant to go to the new vineyard of the Lord, my next assignment. However, since it was the Father's will, I went.

I paused to gather more thoughts, reaching in to my inner self. As I did, I shifted my gaze from my laptop to the painting on the left hand side wall. It was Rembrandt's *The Return of the Prodigal Son*. I looked at it with deep sadness. Unlike the prodigal son in the painting, it pained me to think that I would not be coming back to my old home. Not as a pastor.

I wrote further: *Since this is my last mass in which I am most privileged to celebrate with you as I did over the last ten years, I say goodbye to you. As I go, I thank you for loving me, for praying for me, for assisting and supporting me as your pastor and coworker in this vineyard of the Lord, St. Barnabas parish. Through the years, we planted crops, nurtured them, and harvested fruits, which we offered so generously at masses. They were fruits of our labor, so acceptable to the Lord; fruits of our service shared with others in our spiritual and corporal works of mercy; fruits of our love giving joyful witnesses of who we are and what we do as a holy and healthy parish.*

After typing away words of goodbye, fatigue took hold of me. I guessed both psychological and physical tensions over the last three days had exerted too much pressure on me to the point that I had no choice but to call it a day. So, I decided to finish my homily upon my return to St. Barnabas.

Upon my return late the next day, I resumed writing. When I entered the church, once again, my eyes scanned the encircled icons and images depicting the missionary works of Paul and Barnabas in Southern Asia Minor along the Mediterranean. I have seen those icons many times before. But this time, I appreciated them more than ever before and longed to cling to them for as long as I could. I examined the multicolored mosaic in blue, white, and dark brown on the floor. The crafted stones shaped like a book reminded me of the Book of the Gospel containing the Good News preached by Paul and Barnabas from AD 45–50. The pattern of stones spread out like the islands of Cyprus, Pamphylia, Pisidia, and Lycaonia on the mosaic reminded me of the places where the two did their missionary work. The waves signified the waters of the Mediterranean Sea where the missionaries journeyed over. The center of the mosaic showed the trireme, an ancient Greco-Roman ship with three banks of oars, depicting the vessel used by Paul and Barnabas. At the center of the boat was a white sail hoisted on a wooden cross, an icon representing the Holy Spirit that propelled the ministry of Paul and Barnabas.

Before the Blessed Sacrament, I fell on my knees writing on the armrest of the kneeler: *I thank my brother priests, the parish staff, and leaders of parish organizations who served with me. Most of all, I thank you, the parishioners of St. Barnabas.*

Ten years ago, you welcomed me with open arms. All throughout, I felt the warmth of your loving spirit in my heart and in my soul. You opened your arms and encouraged me to grow more spiritually, both as a person and as your pastor. Your arms so widely open are a constant reminder that they are there to rejoice with me in moments of joy, and to comfort me in moments of sorrow. I cannot thank the Lord enough for you. As I leave, those arms may have closed, not in the wrong gesture of excluding me, but in the gesture of a sweet embrace. As I go to my next assignment, Immaculate Heart of Mary parish in Las Colinas, I take with me your embraces, confident that they will heal me in my woundedness, and lift me up when I'm down. Your sweet embraces, plus your encouraging taps on my back, will speak loudly into my ears, "Well done, faithful servant of the Lord!"

And finally, I wrote the last part of my homily: *I will always be grateful to you for your caring hearts. Through the years, you enabled me to enter a space in your hearts, in your homes, and in your lives. I am truly privileged to have found a home in them. Although I am moving to another place, the home in my heart that you have gifted me with, I will carry around wherever I go, knowing that in this home where the Holy Spirit dwells, will remain forever in mine.*

Let's pray to the Holy Spirit to fill our parish community with His gift of peace. I pray for understanding and wisdom, taking the inspiration from Pope Francis's, "Wisdom is what the Holy Spirit does within us so that we can see everything with God's eyes." Given that, I continue to be a priest in good standing in the Archdiocese of Los Arboles. Please join me in praying for perseverance. I look forward to more years of committed service to the church. I hope and pray that you too will be led by the Holy Spirit, so that you too, as prayed for by Pope Francis, see me, all of me, everything of me with God's eyes. Please pray for me as I do for you. As always, I thank you for your support, and I cherish your friendship. I will miss you all.

8

It was the last week of April 2014, the timely fishing season for local bass, halibut, barracuda, and occasional yellowtail in Southern California. There were about thirty of us anglers who boarded the sports fisher, *Lucky Angler*, for a day of fishing out of Marina del Rey, along the southwesterly shoreline of Los Angeles County.

Raul, my fishing buddy and chair of St. Barnabas Finance Council, suddenly turned to me, spitting words out of frustration. "Father Sal, there must be a better way to deal with what happened to you at St. Barnabas." He waved his hand across my face to get my attention and shook my shoulder with the other hand, expecting to extract a response from me. I parried his hands off me.

Raul's voice sounded rigid. "Those guys in the archdiocese . . . Obviously, they screwed you up."

I pretended not to hear what he said. Something deep within me kept me upset, my thoughts running wild. Something bad happened to me, so why must I allow it to happen to someone else? I must speak out against the evils that have permeated the Archdiocese of Los Arboles.

"Sorry," he apologized. "I know you're preoccupied."

I applied sunscreen to my face and neck. Then I rolled up the sleeves of my T-shirt printed with a fish skeleton and "Catch and

Eat" on the front, for some spray on my arms as well. As I passed the canister to Raul, I felt the warm moisture of the spring breeze on my arm as I handed it to him. He sprayed a generous wisp of mist on his face and his legs. Then he tossed it back to me in no wasted time.

Momentarily, we didn't say a word to each other. We simply stood side by side at the bow of the sports fisher. We leaned against the railing of the boat, basking in the sun, my fingers pressed against the tip of my Dodgers baseball cap, keeping it in place against wind. The fishing destination loomed on the horizon. I took my hand off my cap and called out, pointing and cheering, "Catalina Island, here we come!"

Instead, Raul looked the other way. His eyes followed the trajectory of my blown away cap midway in the air, landing on the water, being swept away by the waves. "How are you to celebrate the Dodgers on their next World Series Championship?" he teased. I blushed, then rubbed the top of my head. I felt unprotected from the midmorning sun.

I sprayed more bursts of sunscreen on my face. I made sure the valve was open before I tossed the canister overboard. It dropped, floating along the whitecaps trailing the boat, spraying till it ran out of aerosol. I put my sunglasses on so I didn't have to squint at the sun, and so that no one else other than Raul could see my eyes bare the turmoil inside of me. Slowly, I walked away, moving toward the galley. But before I could make the first stride, I felt a hand at the back of my shoulder. It was Raul's.

"It's a privilege to spend a day fishing with you." Raul's voice was soothing this time. "Thanks for taking me along. I figure . . . A day like this helps ease your mind. Can we talk?"

I nodded and pointed toward the stern area. "There. A good place to talk about things."

As we walked toward the stern, when we were passing by the bait tank, I pointed to the hundreds of bait fish swimming around the corners of the bait tank, instinctively trying to be free. That observed, Raul grabbed my arms with a challenge. "Call up your survival instinct. Use it to offset your misfortune." He then let go of his grip, "Dare now, fishing buddy!"

Having reached the stern area, I was not in the mood to say anything yet. Instead, I watched the waves slap the hull of *Lucky Angler's* bow, making the anchor sway on contact.

"Any word from the archdiocese?" Raul asked, having adjusted his sunglasses, partly hiding his gaze from me.

"No," I sighed, wishing the boat get to the fishing spot sooner.

"Silent treatment game? Come on, Father Sal," Raul said with his hands extended in a gesture of curiosity. He worked at the Long Beach Hilton as an accountant. In our Parish Finance Council meetings, he customarily referred to open communication among supervisors and employees as an ideal work ethic within corporate institutions. It was this practical wisdom of his that led me to appoint him chair of our parish council three years ago. Since then, we've been fishing along the Southern California coast.

"Sacred silence originates from religious institutions," I flared up. I felt my face turn red. I shook my head. "Sacred silence is not as we ordinarily understand it . . . as meditation or quiet retreat."

"I love retreats," Raul beamed with pride. Then he frowned, "but you just threw a curve ball on me."

I glanced behind the stern, at the wake of whitecaps trailing the boat's twin engines. Shifting my gaze on Raul's furrowed brow, I told him that sacred silence refers to forms, practices, and behavior of violence perpetuated by religious authorities, imposed on the people, disguised as service for the good of the church and the salvation of souls.

"I never thought of it before," Raul said.

"It takes time to let the idea sink into our minds," I said, tapping Raul's arms. Then I explained to him that silence is where perpetrators of crimes hide. That in the case of clergy abuse of minors, perpetrators make sure that the terrified victims are absolutely harassed into silence as well, where the victims have no choice but to keep silent under the gripping climate of fear. "Unfortunately," I summed up, "for some people, silence seems to be the safest and most prudent option."

The boat was getting closer to the "Dome," a favorite fishing spot off Catalina Island, named as such because of its rounded rock formation. I tapped Raul's shoulder. "Let's go fish."

Minutes passed. *Lucky Angler* circled the fishing spot where seagulls swooped down on a ball of bait fish.

"Guys," the skipper announced over the PA system, "school of fish under the birds!" Then the skipper ordered the deckhands, "Chum up! Chum up! Chum up!" One of the two deckhands immediately grabbed a bait net, scooped dozens of live anchovies from the bait tank, and tossed them over to the boiling school of fish. The school of fish went on a feeding frenzy over the chummed bait fish.

The anxious anglers reached for their fishing rods, eager to make their first cast. I grabbed my surface iron rod. The boat's engine sputtered to a gradual halt. The boat idled, drifting.

"I'll watch you," Raul deferred.

I clicked the reel gear to free spool and poised my rod to a casting position. The surface iron jig dangled halfway between the reel and the tip of the rod.

"Let go, guys!" the skipper ordered excitedly.

"*Swisssssshhhhhh*," sounded my line peeling off the reel as I fired the jig away. The jig flew out in a curve-ball trajectory toward the water.

"Hook up!" yelled one of the deckhands who was standing by the bait tank, intermittently tossing chum overboard. "At the stern," he called out, pointing to my bent rod.

I reeled in the hooked fish as it zigzagged its way toward the corner from where I was fishing.

"You're a fisherman, fisher of men!" Raul gasped, his mouth wide-opened in wonderment as I unhooked the thirty-some-inch slimy barracuda.

"Your turn," I said, catching my breath, handing him my rod.

"I can't cast."

I took the rod back from him, cut the jig off the monofilament, and knotted a dropper loop. I pulled a sinker and a circle hook from the front pocket of my Levi's, attached them to the line, and handed the rod back to him.

"Bait it up with a live anchovy. Go for a keeper halibut. It has to be at least twenty-two inches."

Raul slid the line down to the water. He clicked the reel gear to lock position when the sinker hit the bottom. Minutes passed. No action below the surface, not even a nibble. The school of hungry barracudas had left the spot.

"According to René Girard, a historian and philosopher, 'sacred' has a double connotation of holiness and blood-shedding," I whispered to Raul, hoping that the no-bite situation did not dampen his spirit. "Holiness and blood-shedding are like the two sides of a coin."

"Watch your language, Father," Raul cautioned me, obviously not disappointed that he was not getting a bite. "You're mean to that poor 'cuda." He saw that the treble, razor-sharp hooks of my jig ripped the fish's mouth and that the fish bled profusely at the tip of the deckhand's gaff. By that, he commented that some guys in the archdiocese seemed to be more violent to me than I was to the fish.

"Sports fishing is a socially accepted recreation," I rationalized. "It includes bloodshed."

"What do you mean?" Raul asked with a quizzical look. I invited him over to the galley for a cold beer.

Seated in the galley, both of us drinking Bud Light, I explained to Raul that the dual connotation of sacred is illustrated both in the Old Testament and in the New Testament of the Bible. That in the Old Testament, for example, Aaron, the high priest, on the Day of Atonement, slaughtered bullocks and goats to symbolically lay the sins of the people on the altar of sacrifice.

"But," Raul objected, "such sacrifice could be misunderstood, I mean, about what has been going on . . ."

"No. Not in the cases where minors are abused at the hands of priests." I explained further that in the New Testament, Jesus Christ, the sacrificial Lamb and the high priest, offered himself as the sin offering once for all.

"Are you referring to the sacrifice of the mass?" he asked.

"Yes. And by the way, in the Bible, the act of sacrificing is a sacred ritual. The victim has to undergo violence first before it becomes a fitting and acceptable sacrifice. The scapegoat, as the sacrificial offering, is purposely set aside to be slaughtered on behalf of and for the sake of the people."

"Blood! Is that what is all about?" Raul took issue, looking nauseated. I guess he had been watching the deckhands scrub off fish blood from the deck.

"True," I confirmed. "As Jesus hung on the cross, a Roman soldier pierced his side with a lance. Blood and water flowed out from him. At mass, wine and water are mixed to make a perfect sacrifice."

I saw Raul's face turn bluish. His breathing was hard, short, and rapid.

"Did you take Dramamine an hour before we left the dock?" I asked, concerned.

"I did. But this nasty thing called sacred silence on the part of church leaders, their violence, and scapegoating make me feel like throwing up."

"When our church leaders refuse to deal with issues that are brought to their attention, when they refuse to respond, others throw up too."

"It makes me sick . . ." Raul said out of breath, balancing himself against the rail. ". . . at the thought that church leaders cannibalize their own." Then he threw up, both out of seasickness and disgust.

I assisted him as he walked to the sundeck, to the corner where the life jackets were stowed. He spent the rest of the day on the heap of life jackets, sleeping off seasickness while I continued fishing until I had caught ten barracudas, the legal limit for a day. On the way back to the dock, I gave a modest tip to the deckhand to fillet them for me.

Back at the dock, I handed the filleted fish to Raul, adding my telegraphic culinary instructions, "Marinate with Italian dressing. Medium well on the grill. Tastes better with beer."

9

Something unusual happened at the meeting in the parish hall on April 8, 2014. Soller arranged that meeting for members of St. Barnabas Finance Council, Pastoral Council, and parish staff. A group of fifteen people participated.

"Father Sal, I didn't expect you to be here," Soller, who was standing at the entrance of the parish hall, said in his usual condescending tone of voice as he spotted me. He knew that I was already out of St. Barnabas, assigned as priest-in-residence in Immaculate Heart of Mary in Las Colinas.

"I'm not a gate-crasher," I asserted. "Raul invited me."

Sally, a retired Afro American schoolteacher in her late 60s, and the chair of St. Barnabas Pastoral Council, had arranged the chairs in a semicircle for the members and one for the bishop at the top. She called the meeting to order and immediately called the bishop to speak. The bishop blankly stared at the participants and clicked his fingers like a magician calling himself out of nowhere.

"Father Sal's term of office has expired. So . . . He has to go. Vow of obedience, you know," Soller chattered like a Pinocchio coming out of a box.

At the other end of the hall, near the kitchen, the aroma of the brewing coffee and freshly baked chocolate chip cookies, prepared by one of the parish council members, wafted over the parish hall. But it didn't distract the participants from what Soller had just said.

Suddenly, I heard something which I never heard before at parish meetings.

"Boo . . . boo . . . boo . . ." a collective sound of defiance from the parish staff and leaders filled the hall. They stomped their feet on the floor. Then they stood up, one after another, turned to me, cheering, and said, "Father Sal, Father Sal, we're with you."

Soller shrugged and threw his hands up in the air. I sensed outrage among the parish leaders. One of them was Rex, a canon lawyer and a member of our Parish Council. Rex and I knew each other since our seminary days in the '60s. He left the seminary right after our college graduation to study Canon Law at Catholic University of America where he earned his JCD degree. He then moved to Los Angeles. He sported long hair and a "Che" Guevara cap. I once asked him why the long hair and the hat. He replied with a wink, "The world is in perpetual revolution," alluding to the anti-establishment movement in the '60s.

Rex could not hold his peace. "Father Sal, did you file an administrative recourse to delay the implementation of the archbishop's decision?" he asked. "You should have done it within ten days after you were removed."

"I was neither made aware of it, nor given the time to file it," I replied.

Rex confronted Soller. "You could have done better reminding Father Sal of his rights. But as of today, the provision had expired. You tricked him."

Sally spoke, facing the group, "Father Sal deserved to be given sufficient time to move out. As is my practice as president of our home owner association, the board and I give at least two weeks' notice before evicting renters."

"In retrospect," Raul surmised, "I now see why Bishop Soller did what he did. To make sure that Father Sal couldn't taste the flavor of the law. For this, we're holding Bishop Soller accountable."

"Our meeting tonight is not about canonical matters," Soller insisted, clearly showing his impatience. He eyed Raul momentarily, then gave him a dismissive wave.

"So, if it's not about our pastor's rights," Rex spoke up in spite of Soller's rudeness, "then *what* is this meeting all about?"

Soller circled his head in the air, spaced out. "It is, aaah . . . It's to inform you, the staff, and the parish leaders that we have decided to send you a new pastor."

I didn't waste a second to take a shot at Soller. "On paper, I'm not any longer the pastor, but my relationship with the parishioners as their shepherd continues."

"Pipe down!" Soller barked like a drill sergeant.

I was not intimidated. Nor were the parish staff and parish leaders. On the contrary, they stood up, and a barrage of questions ensued.

"What is the *real* reason why our pastor was removed?" Sally engaged Soller, who was the only one seated. She closed in on him in a menacing stance.

"Because of administrative and financial issues," Soller answered. "Over a period of time, the parish owes the archdiocese the amount of over two hundred thousand dollars in assessments."

"Why abruptly?" Raul chimed in as he moved to stand next to Sally. "You just don't know how outrageous this is to the parishioners. Your impulsive decision-making is nightmarish, to say the least."

"Why did you not follow the proper procedure?" Rex blurted out, pointing his finger straight at Soller's nose. "You should have informed our pastor well in advance before taking him out." He held up the pages from the archdiocesan handbook containing the policy on pastors' change of assignment. I knew that Rex had the facts all laid out. I've read the handbook many times over during my years as pastor. The Placement Board's policy specified that pastors whose term of office ends on the following year are to be informed of the forthcoming change in September of the previous year. "Your statement about administrative and financial issues attributed to our pastor is obnoxious, given that you yourself don't follow rules," Rex surmised.

"At work, employees are given at least a two-week notice," Raul stated. "Why don't we all learn from their employers?" His eyes narrowed on Soller, accompanied by a verbal lash. "You're just plain cruel. You often speak of mercy, but where's *your* heart?"

"Too much politics in the church!" Rex added, glaring at Soller. "You wield too much power, and you use it to engage the archdiocesan staff to form a conspiracy against our pastor."

"If you only knew—" Soller said, dragging his words but did not finish the sentence.

"*Sayang, kapwang Filipino pa naman,*" Raul sighed out loud, lamenting Soller's lack of sensitivity for his fellow countryman.

Raul then turned to Sally, commenting in a way that everyone in the room heard, "He *really* has an attitude."

I saw Sally tap Raul's arm, then I heard her say to him in an affirming voice, "You're not alone in this."

Raul rolled his eyes and commented, "I wonder who will be the next *kababayan*, countryman, he will throw under the bus."

The other participants, too disturbed to speak up, dropped their heads down. They left without saying a word. The meeting ended prematurely. Coffee and cookies that were laid out on the snack table were left untouched.

10

The following weekend after that unsettling meeting in the parish hall, Soller, at his own insistence, announced my departure at all the masses. Sally, who was at one of the masses, called me up that Sunday night.

"By the way, I saw Father Clem at mass in St. Barnabas this morning. One of my friends from our parish told me you are friends."

"Yes, we are."

"Changing the subject, is it true that you *did* step down? Bishop Soller announced to parishioners at all the masses that you did. They're confused."

"No, I didn't step down," I replied. "Soller made it sound that I had to." Muscles around my Adam's apple tightened momentarily. I pressed the hold button on my phone.

"Father? Are you? Still there?"

I pressed the hold button back to talk mode, lamenting, "I was removed without due process."

"Due process?"

I explained to Sally that in Canon Law, before issuing a singular decree, the bishop is to seek out the necessary information and proofs and to hear those whose rights can be injured. Pastors have the right to their good name. Before someone is judged, the accusers must have a founded belief, a semblance of truth, that the accused was involved in the commission of a crime."

"In your case, what should have been the right process?"

I explained to her further that two important processes could have been engaged in. The first one is for the accusers to prove that I caused grave damage to the church. Second, assuming that the specific problem had been named, the accusers had to determine that it could not be remedied in any other way. Otherwise, in my case, an arrangement should have been made for temporal administration, and I be left to carry out most of my pastoral duties.

"I'm upset," Sally said, hyperventilating. "Bishop Soller made it appear as if you were convicted of a crime so heinous—like sexual abuse of minors."

"I'd go to jail if that were the case."

"You're not," Sally objected. "You're not part of that rubbish."

I heard Sally's heavy breathing, then her question, "So, what other scenario could be considered in your case?"

"I explained to her further that in some cases, a pastor is removed because his pastoral ministry has become ineffective. Whether or not the pastor in question is culpable, efforts must be made on the part of the bishop to assist, rather than remove, an otherwise effective pastor whose administration of finances has caused serious harm to the church. The bishop must conduct an inquiry to his satisfaction that the pastor's ministry has become ineffective.

"I did my best. I showed due diligence in my responsibilities as a pastor."

"Did Archbishop Fernandez and Bishop Soller ever consider what you just explained to me?"

"No. Neither did they persuade me to resign in fifteen days as provided for in Canon Law."

"I have known you all these years. I worked side by side with you. With members of the Pastoral Council, together, we visualized and initiated our parish priorities of evangelization, community-building, and stewardship. So, what's the problem?"

"Clericalism," I quickly replied. Then I explained to Sally what I meant by it, telling her that Soller, whose imputed power and authority derived from ordination, used his position and power to control rather than lead the people of God in the light of the Gospel. That Soller kicked me out of the parish and out of his region. That the saying, "Give a man a gun and a uniform and he can be an outright killer or an assassin," plus my own version of it, "Give a man a miter and a staff, and he will indulge in scapegoating revelries," applied to Soller's character.

"It's unfortunate that church leaders institutionalize the evils of clericalism," Sally sighed, her voice muffled over the receiver.

"After the mass," she added, "I saw parishioners approach Bishop Soller, perhaps to ask him what he did to you. Soller just walked away from them."

"I pity the parishioners for being deprived of the truth they have the right to know. In Soller's case, professionalism takes a backseat to his impulsiveness. He must put the good of the people ahead of his ego. His credibility's at stake."

"There's an urgency to speak out about this," Sally verbalized her inner thought. "But to whom?"

"The people of God have the right to communicate with their bishop, as provided for in canon law," I offered.

"I thought so too." Sally said confidently. "I spoke with some leaders of our parish. Some of them suggested going open in the media. Others suggested picketing in font of the Archdiocesan Catholic Center. What do you think?"

"To me, the best way is to ask yourselves which way is the most effective, given this particular situation."

"You're speaking in parables, Father," Sally commented. "You kind of take the high road."

"Talk to someone. Or, have you already figured it out?"

"Letter writing!" Sally's voice exploded over the phone. "I'll talk to parish leaders."

"I'll talk to my friends and family members as well."

"Deal," Sally's voice sounded relaxed, committed.

I noticed that my iPhone had registered several minutes of talk time. "Thanks for your call, Sally," I hinted at concluding the conversation. "Talk to you soon."

"Bye for now, Father Sal."

11

A month later, Sally hosted a potluck dinner-meeting of parish leaders in her house to go over the letters sent to the officials of the Archdiocese of Los Arboles. I brought halibut fillets, which I grilled at Sally's barbecue pit a few minutes before dinner. Others brought soft drinks, appetizers, Pollo Loco chicken, guacamole and chips, and rice. Raul brought a six-pack of Corona beer. Rex brought a placard with the inscription, "To Set the Captives Free," in reference to the liberation theology movement of the '70s. With Sally's instruction, he taped it on the wall of the living room where we would have our meeting.

At the end of dinner, Sally invited everyone over to have a seat in the living room. She took the floor and announced that due to the efforts of the members of both Parish Council and Finance Council, approximately 50 personal letters from priests and lay leaders were sent to Archbishop Fernandez and Bishop Soller. The letters focused on the issue of and requested an explanation of why I was removed from St. Barnabas and why so abruptly.

"First things first, though." Sally called the group's attention to my baseball cap emblazoned on the front with *St. Barnabas Fish Fry*. "Let's hear from our fisherman-turned-cook."

"About Fish Fry?" I asked jokingly. I looked around and saw faces with wide smiles.

"The Knights of Columbus and I raise funds to take schoolchildren for a day of fishing. I grill my freshly caught fillets of fish, and the Knights serve them at dinner in the parish hall."

"At a discounted price, I suppose," Rex commented, "yet, you raise enough funds for a good cause."

"It works every time," I said proudly. I saw heads nod in agreement.

"Father, share with us now . . . letters from your friends," Sally requested.

"Needless to say, I have been encouraged by your support. My priest-friend who is a pastor in San Francisco told me he sent his letter to the archbishop and Soller. He asked me to share it with you. Let me read it to you: *'Five days to get out of the parish that one has dedicated himself zealously for more than ten years is unheard of in my thirty-eight years as a priest. Father Galvez is not perfect, but from my long-standing friendship with him for over fifty-one years, I will definitely say that he is a person and a priest I have deep respect for. I consider him my stellar ideal of what priests should be nowadays when we are attacked from all sides, even from within the church.'"

Sally and two other parish leaders approached me, and one after another hugged me without saying a word.

"Sadly," I exclaimed as I folded the letter, "my friend said no one responded to his letter."

"I too wrote a letter to Archbishop Fernandez, cc. Bishop Soller," said Raul. He had his hand up, his other hand holding an almost empty Corona. Sally called him up to read from a copy of his letter. Raul did. "*For the short notice to vacate, Father Galvez was treated unkindly and without compassion. This made me question my faith in the leadership of the Catholic Church in the San Pio Region. How can you look at the eyes of the thousands of people from whom you keep asking for donations at the Sunday services on weekends, when you yourselves do not practice what you preach? It's a shame. Now I understand why the attendance in the Catholic Church is diminishing. When you preach about compassion in your archdiocese, do you really mean it in your heart?"*

"Double standard," Rex commented. His face flushed red. Turning to Raul, he asked, "What merit did you get for sticking your neck out for Father Sal?"

"I never got a response," Raul sighed, hardly keeping his cool, gulping the last ounce of beer, and then he tossed the empty can into the trash.

"I also wrote to Archbishop Fernandez, cc. Bishop Soller," Sally announced. She read from a Xerox copy of her original, "*Our family has been parishioners of St. Barnabas parish for twenty-five years and has seen priests get transferred to other parishes. This time, the process of removing Father Sal was wrong. It was handled poorly. We were devastated and saddened. What was done was disrespectful, not just to Father Sal, but also to us, parishioners."*

The uncomfortable silence was broken by the heavy breathing among the parish group. Sally shielded her own breathing by walking over to the food table and picked up a saucer to fill it with Doritos chips and guacamole.

"So, where's the compassion, especially from the religious people like them?" Sally took it up again. "They're supposed to be role models to the community, and we're supposed to look up to them like the way we look up to Jesus, who is full of compassion, respect, and is forgiving. We pray to God that this kind of unchristian occurrence won't happen again to anybody, especially to religious people like Father Sal."

As soon as Sally finished talking, Rex asked whether she got any response from either one of the church officials.

"*Nada*," Sally attested, burying a handful of chips into the dip and gobbling them up, making the conversation spicier.

"You're all fired up, Sally," Rex declared.

"Someone put too much chili in the guacamole," she complained.

Rex turned to Raul. "No better combination than a cold beer and a marinated filet of fish, right?"

"Right," Raul confirmed. "Father Sal taught me that mantra. At sea and on land."

There was a bit of relief, but it didn't last.

"I also engaged Archbishop Fernandez and Bishop Soller," Rex spoke up. "And I too wrote them a letter. I'll read part of it. '*I have listened to some parishioners who have expressed surprise by the abrupt removal of Father Sal. Most of them are familiar with the diocesan policy of pastor's term of office, and they expected the changing of the guard to happen in 2016 when the term of Father Sal should have terminated as a matter of course.*'"

Rex's tone of voice shifted from his ordinary guttural to a high pitch, letting go of the paper he was reading from, his fists balled up. He pounded on the sides of his seat, "Parishioners cannot comprehend. Many cannot accept why their pastor's assignment was aborted before coming to full term. If Bishop Soller's statement that Father Sal's term had ended in 2010, why was it not renewed then? Why was not the nonrenewal put in writing and communicated to Father Sal? Did it mean that for four years, Father Sal was not their pastor? Whose duty was it to write the official renewal, and why was it not done? Why was the assignment terminated midway of the supposed second term? Bishop Soller could have spared Father Sal and the parishioners volumes of pain."

The parish leaders nodded in agreement with Rex. They blushed as they shifted their gaze from Rex to each other. Rex stood up, turned to the placard on the wall, and pondered on its message. "I can't say enough about it." He sat back down with downcast eyes.

Raul raised his hand, requesting to speak. Sally nodded to acknowledge him.

"Rex is a close friend of Father Sal's family," Raul stated. "I understand that Father's family, like our parish family, is undergoing so much pain as well."

"So, then," Sally surmised, "let us, the parish leaders, assign Rex to reach out to Father's family." Turning to Rex, she said, "Will you?"

"Will do," Rex gladly responded, his voice now back to normal, his hands relaxed, his head up.

12

A week later, after the dinner hosted by my sister, Miriam, and her husband, Nazario, my family gathered in the living room for a conversation with Rex, whom we consider adopted family member.

Rex spoke, as if in a prologue of a melodrama, "The abrupt removal of Father Sal, rather than create a smooth transition between pastors and peace in the parish, has, in fact, caused bewilderment and perplexing questions among parishioners." He cleared his throat and then explained to the family that, in this particular case, the archbishop would not want this atmosphere of conflict and confusion among the grieving family members. That this kind of sudden and stringent procedure was usually resorted to generally for those who have been determined to be reasonably guilty of a crime, civil or canonical.

"But why, why this?" Miriam mumbled, hyperventilating.

"Good question," Rex responded, "but I cannot honestly answer that. Bishop Soller's statement gives the assurance that this is not the situation. Yet, in another line, he insinuates that there seems to be some shadow of an anomaly."

"What is it?" Miriam insisted, "We are entitled to know the truth."

"True," Rex said. "The truth is Father Sal, for his many years of dedicated service, deserves more humane treatment, to say the least." Rex paused momentarily, then picked up in a menacing tone of voice, "It will serve Bishop Soller's good name if he prepared for damage control."

I spoke up, holding up the copies of letters from our family's priest-relatives serving in the Philippines. I related to the family members that Monsignor Hector, Father Allen, and my two nephews, Fr. Lou and Fr. Hal, wrote a letter to Archbishop Fernandez, cc. Bishop Soller, expressing their deepest sympathy for me. They made a joint statement saying that the means by which I was removed from the parish lacked the sensitivity of *solidaritas in presbyterio* (solidarity in the priesthood).

"Did Fernandez and Soller respond to their letter?" Rex inquired with keen interest.

I told the group that according to Monsignor Hector in our overseas phone conversation, Archbishop Fernandez didn't, but Bishop Soller did on behalf of the archbishop. Monsignor Hector further told me that in Soller's letter to our priest-relatives, he assured them that his decision was tempered with prayer, objectivity, and compassion, that his decision was not for any selfish motive but solely for the greater good of brother priests and the greater benefit of the people entrusted to his pastoral care.

"Sounds like it's coming from a whitened sepulcher," I commented, delighting on the confirming nods of my relatives.

"I also wrote letters," my mother, Clara, who never said a word at dinner, finally spoke up. She pulled out a copy of her handwritten letter.

"Read it aloud," the surprised family members said in unison.

My mother put on her reading glasses and slowly read her own handwriting. "*Dear Archbishop Fernandez and Bishop Soller, I am the ninety-five-year-old mother of Father Galvez, my only son, whom I offered to love and serve God and His people as a priest. Recently, I don't have peace of mind due to what happened to him as pastor of St. Barnabas. He informed us, his family, that he was ordered to move to another location outside. If he has done something not right, I think you should be his best support. As a mother, I too am here to help him in any way possible. The sad situation is that there is no ready official assignment he could transfer to. He had to look for a church that will accept him as a priest in residence. I am feeling what he is feeling now.*"

"We, his family, offered him a place to stay for a while," Miriam interjected.

All eyes were on me, expecting a confirmation of Miriam's statement.

"Since ordination, I have chosen to belong to the church family. So I must make the church my home."

"That we understand," Rex said, as a matter-of-fact. "So, now, let's give back the floor to Mother." All agreed.

My mom resumed reading, "*. . . My daily prayers for him and other priests have been the chalice of strength, so I have to continue praying in the remaining days of my life until I reach the sunset of my life in this world. I hope and pray that the same situation will not happen to other priests in the future.*"

I saw her tears drop on the page. My mother reached for her handkerchief. I looked around. I saw everyone's eye moisten.

"I'm going to keep this copy and place it between the pages of my prayer book, right on the page where I pray my daily prayer for priests," my mother said as she folded her letter. In front of the pages, she inserted a holy card.

"Our Lady of Guadalupe," I commented about the holy card. "It came from Archbishop Fernandez."

"By the way . . ." Rex said. He stood up, reached for my mother's arm, tapping it sympathetically. ". . . did Archbishop Fernandez and Bishop Soller respond to your letter?"

"The archbishop did not, but Bishop Soller did," my mother said with a confused look.

I looked around me. I noticed similar confused look on the faces of my family members. "Tell us. Bishop Soller's response," was again the family members communal request.

"I don't know what to make out of this," my mother said reluctantly as she pulled out a page from another envelope printed with an official logo.

"Read it. For everyone to know," Rex said with pronounced urgency.

"All right. Here it is," our mother complied. "Bishop Soller addressed me as 'Mrs. Galvez.'"

"Go ahead, don't put us in suspense," was again the family members' insistence.

"All right . . ." our mother read the paragraph, "*As a bishop and leader of the church, I always try my best to treat my fellow priests as brothers in ministry with fraternal affection and respect. I am very aware of my serious responsibility as a 'father' to my brother priests—called to care for and support each and every one of them.*"

After my mom finished reading, I observed that my family members turned to each other, their faces grimacing with disgust. They shook their heads, shaking off Soller's double talk.

"Do you plan to put that letter between the pages of your prayer book too?" Rex inquired, attempting some comic relief.

"It does not belong there," my mom replied.

My sisters, Miriam, Camelia, and Laura, also wrote to Archbishop

Fernandez and Bishop Soller. They received form letters from Soller, the same form letter he wrote in response to my mother's first hand-written letter.

"I wrote letters too," Nazario, my brother-in-law confided.

"And so did I," Ildefonso, my other brother-in-law seconded.

"About requesting a meeting with us," my brothers-in-law said as if in a duet.

"Did anyone respond?" Rex inquired.

"No," they said simultaneously.

"Perhaps the officials of the archdiocese will respond to a civil suit," Nazario threw a challenge to the group. His challenge came as a surprise to me. For someone who in his younger years did not have the opportunity to practice his faith, but currently was catching up by reading faith-based books and watching religious-themed television programs, Nazario's respect for the institutional church seemed to be diminishing.

"On what grounds?" Rex tested Nazario.

"For harassment," Nazario asserted. "At work, cases involving harassment are sure winners."

Rex initiated a high-five with him. "As family members, you have the right to sue the archdiocese."

"Hold on," I said, acting like a pooper. "I really don't go for it. In spite of the reprehensible actions of church officials, I still believe that our church's mission remains sacred."

"Oh, I forgot to tell you," my mother spoke again. "I told Bishop Soller about his harassment of Father Sal."

"And?" was the curious reaction from the family members.

"He denied it," my mom murmured. "I wrote a second letter," my mother announced. She raised a copy for everyone to see.

"I can see from here that you handwrote it too. You're showing

LORETO N. GONZALES JR.

off your calligraphic skills," Rex declared, pursuing his attempt at comic relief.

"I did," my mother acknowledged. "I told Archbishop Fernandez and Bishop Soller that I believed it was necessary to say, in the name of the Lord, what I felt, and must listen with humility and accept God's will. I told them that they are the only ones who can clarify this situation on behalf of my son. I trusted them to give an explanation to give me peace of mind in the remaining days of my life. I promised them to continue praying and to keep hoping that I could see them personally before I finally leave this world and be at peace with God."

No one else dared to say anything.

"Neither did the archbishop nor the bishop respond to my second letter," my mother recounted.

13

I was in Soller's office for a meeting he called that day in the fall of 2014. It was November 2nd, All Souls Day, the day Catholics around the world set aside in remembrance of their faithful departed.

"Archbishop Fernandez received your application letter for the pastorate of St. Ignatius. The archbishop had accepted my recommendation *not* to make you a pastor again," Soller declared.

"Why?" I asked. "The very same day you got rid of me, you told me to apply for a pastorate at a later time. I believed the time had come."

Soller absentmindedly glanced at the live screen of his laptop laid out on the corner of his desk. Lately, he had developed the habit of doing so and carried the laptop around at meetings.

"Did I say that?" He took his eyes off the computer screen, looking innocent.

"You did. I keep brief documentations of our meetings." I pulled out a flash drive from my shirt pocket to show it to him. "They're all here."

"They're all here too," Soller beamed, tapping his fingers on the laptop. "But we are not going your way."

"*Contra factum non valet argumentum,*" I recited in Latin. "Your word against mine." I put the flash drive back into my pocket, then paused to catch my breath before I stated, "Over the last few months, I spent time praying for healing. I also sought spiritual direction at St. John Vianney House of Prayer. Are these . . . exercises in futility?"

"You have not complied with the requirement to go through a psychological evaluation. In line with the policy that governs priests such as in your *special* circumstances, you needed to prove your readiness and worthiness to serve as pastor. But in defiance, you tore up the therapist's calling card. We don't have any record from any therapist that you've attended anger management."

"You instructed me to see a psychotherapist, but you didn't bother going yourself. Victims and perpetrators are two sides of the coin, as we all know."

"I don't need to go. But it's *you* who needed to spend time patching the division you caused in the church. You turned the parish leaders, your friends, and your family against the church. You wasted too much time being on the wrong side of the fence."

"It's not wasted time seeking the advice of Rex, my canon lawyer." I told Soller that in my sessions with him, we talked about my rights to an impartial decision-making, to adequate notice, to be heard, to assistance and representaton, to an equitable decision and remedies.

"We have our own canon lawyers. I don't give credence to outsiders."

"Rex specializes in bishop-priest conflicts."

"Even more so . . ." Soller trailed off. "You, you veered off the tracks. I'm sure now more than ever that the archbishop and I made the right decision to deny your application."

"Don't scapegoat me!" I said, rising from my seat and wanting to walk away.

"It's not me." Soller pointed me back to my chair.

I sat back and stretched out my hands. I opened wide my palms like a beggar desperately in need of a brother to spare a dime of truth. "What's your standard of evaluation by which I have been prejudged not eligible to be a pastor again?"

"It's not my standard. It's the archdiocese's. You have kept yourself out."

"You're a *bishop*. The priests of the archdiocese and I gave you our vote of confidence."

Having paused to read the framed certificate of appointment on the side wall to the left of his executive chair, I took him to task. "Speak for us without fear of losing your position . . . outside of your drive to get ahead of the ranks."

"My office implements the policies of the archdiocese," Soller declared. "It's final."

"Scavenger!" I blurted out.

I thought of the article I read from one of my fishing magazines about terns. Terns made their nests on branches of mangroves. The laying of eggs was spaced out, and so, the hatching. Out of struggle for survival and competition for the parents' attention, the older and stronger siblings pushed the younger ones out of the nest, over the water, to drown.

Convinced that I was pushed out by the church officials to drown, instead of speaking up to register my protest, I gathered my saliva and spat on the floor. Then I left with a heavy heart, not just because I felt cheated but because other priests I knew felt the same way. I placed my hand over my heart that was racing with rage. As I did, I felt a pounding of sorts—the digital content of my documentations. I pulled the flash drive out. Before I made the first step to leave, I turned to Soller, holding the flash drive up. "What about this?"

"We'll take it up at our next meeting," he promised. But what I heard was a promise . . . again . . . made to be broken.

14

A week passed.

Father Clem and I were taking a walk around the premises of St. John Vianney House of Prayer, a retreat house for the priests of the Archdiocese of Los Arboles. We scheduled a day together for a day of recollection so we could also have a chance to catch up with each other.

"For some strange reason, I attended the mass at St. Barnabas," Father Clem said, recalling that day on March 2014. "Then I heard Bishop Soller announce that the pastor stepped down because of some kind of financial issues. At first, I didn't believe he was referring to you."

"You heard it too?" I asked, surprised. "That's what friends are for . . . They've got each other's back," I said in a soothing tone.

"I was on sick leave from St. Perpetua's. One of my friends from St. Barnabas invited me to attend mass there. I planned to say hi to you, but my friend said you were gone."

Father Clem's assignment at St. Perpetua started twenty-two years ago as an associate pastor. In 2000, Cardinal O'Malley appointed him pastor. Twelve years later, Archbishop Fernandez renewed his appointment, to end in September 2018.

"I heard you got sick, sorry," I offered. "When do you plan to return to St. Perpetua's?"

"No word about it yet. I was put on sick leave to regain full recovery from a nonlife-threatening condition. Bishop Soller visited me in the hospital and told me that as soon as I recovered, I was to return to St. Perpetua to resume my duties as pastor. Last month, my doctors told me that I was healthy enough to go back to work. Since then, I've been ready and able to assume my former duties as pastor."

"So, what's holding you back?"

"Bishop Soller broke his promise. Behind my back, he arranged for the appointment of Father Herbert as the administrator of St. Perpetua."

Clem lightly elbowed me. He put his hand over his mouth and said in a whisper, "Bishop Soller loves to golf." He then made motions in the air, sketching a master and a dog on leash. "He got Father Herbert as his caddy. Which means, my return is uncertain."

We strolled along the cobble-stoned pavement lined with pine trees. The marble statue of St. John Vianney, patron saint of diocesan priests, loomed in front of us. A wooden bench was set in place in front of the statue. I imagined that it was placed on purpose for the priests on retreat so they could make it their habit to contemplate on St. John Vianney's priestly virtues.

"How do you feel about it?" I asked, setting my footsteps toward the statue, alerting Clem to the direction we could take.

As we walked along, Clem confided to me that the unnecessary and prolonged delay for his return to active ministry was agonizing, to say the least. He explained to me that he had been in a constant struggle to keep his chin up, and the level of his disappointment, frustration, restlessness, and anxiety had risen quite high. He said that he was preoccupied with the recurring thought of whether he *can* return to work. That the thought itself was torture, stressing him out, causing loss of sleep, and taking away the joy of friends, food, and games, not to mention the zest for prayer and spiritual matters.

By then, we had reached the statue. We stood in front of it, admiring the artist's depiction of a nineteenth-century French priest known for his exemplary pastoral ministry. I stepped forward and touched the base of the statue.

"If we add up our years of service to the archdiocese," I figured, "it could exceed sixty years, between the two of us."

"Pretty much like senior citizens," Clem surmised with a grin, pointing to the half bald head of the statue.

"How are you coasting along, in your present situation? I know it's tough," I asked Clem, who, at the moment, was rubbing his own balding head.

"Patience, of which I used to have much, seems to be running thin. I feel like, without direction to take, my optimism and hope fade little by little on the horizon. I feel hurt, betrayed, abandoned, and let down by my higher-ups as my trust and respect for them begins to dwindle."

When Clem spoke about being betrayed by our superiors and of his trust and respect for them dwindling, I felt something deep inside me resonate with his words.

"I'm so disappointed," I let out, as if exhaling a typical Southern California summer smog. "St. John Vianney's teaching falls on deaf ears. His good examples, surely, on closed eyes." I paused, realizing that Clem had something more to say. "I'm sorry."

"It's okay," Clem said, pointing to St. John Vianney's stole. His voice turned somber. "We, priests, are sworn to serve, but in some cases, our superiors dampen our spirit. And that's exactly how I feel lately. With self-esteem and self-worth going down, I tend now to shy away from fellow priests and parishioners and simply want to be left alone with my growing depression."

"Let's sit on the bench," I suggested to Clem, noticing his voice faltering.

We took a few steps toward the bench, where we sat. A squirrel climbed down from one of the trees. It picked up a pine cone lying on the ground, clasped it, and mischievously displayed it to us as if saying that it felt good to be holding on to one, rather than losing one.

"How about the parishioners? How have the shock waves affected them?" I inquired.

"St. Perpetua parishioners are adversely affected," Clem stated. He then pursued telling me that he called parish leaders for a meeting and a consultation. He enumerated the feedback verbalized by those who participated. The participants claimed that the conditions posed by the archdiocese for his return to St. Perpetua were unfair; that he had being singled out; that the items on the conditions for his reinstatement were solely about money; that he had to seek legal counsel for being harassed; that the present priest-administrator was rumormongering; that he was being investigated without prior charges; that the parishioners were to picket in front of the Archdiocesan Center if nothing else happened.

"Was there a follow-up meeting?" I inquired further.

"None. But to make known their thoughts and feelings, parishioners wrote letters to Archbishop Fernandez, copying Bishop Soller." Clem confided to me that a petition letter with 2,300 signatories for his reinstatement was mailed to Archbishop Fernandez and to Bishop Soller. Clem further confided to me that one of his parishioners wrote to the Apostolic Nuncio, the pope's delegate to the church in U.S., whose office was in Washington, D.C., informing him of Soller's abuse of power.

"Your parishioners did the right thing and connected with the right persons," I commented. "Soller's abuse of power is tantamount to a crime like abuse of minors. In our case, abuse of subordinates."

Clem shared with me more of his observation: Parishioners had been seen attending church services in neighboring parishes, withholding their donation from St. Perpetua's. This, according to him, was the parishioners' way of expressing their disgust and disapproval since their voice as members of God's people were being ignored and not being attended to by their current shepherds with whom they shared the prophetic role.

"So, what do you plan to do?" I asked.

"I already wrote a petition addressed to the archbishop seeking the intermediation of the Board of Consultors to resolve the case at hand in order to give me peace of mind. By doing it, I am not driven by insubordination, personal gain, or passion in taking this step. My entire priestly life and ministry have always been exercised in conformity with the law of the church, which ensures the protection and safeguard of the rights of all members and upholds justice for everyone."

"No response, I suppose."

"None."

"Ouch! Foul! Ouch!" I cried out as if hit in the groin by an invisible mixed martial-arts fighter.

But it hit Clem more than it did me. I did not hear Clem's voice momentarily. I took a side glimpse on his belly, imagining a bursting bagpipe. No, it was his whole self that was bursting with anger. His arms were shaking, let alone his knees.

"Let's walk to the dining room for a drink," I suggested. "A glass of wine won't get us a ticket for drunk-talking."

"Brilliant idea. Let's go," Clem agreed, feeling relieved. "But first,

I need to go to my car to pick up some papers."

A few minutes later, Clem and I were sitting comfortably in the dining room, separate from the small dining room where silent retreatants have their meals.

"The list of conditions that you mentioned a while ago, the ones I assume have the archbishop's tacit concurrence, do you recall what they are?" I asked as we were refreshing ourselves with a glass of merlot.

"I have a good feeling that the document about the archbishop's expectations of me as I return from sick leave to complete my term as pastor of St. Perpetua Church was written by Deacon Schaeffer for Bishop Soller."

"Schaeffer, Soller's clone. What did he say?"

At that, Clem showed me the papers he picked up from his car. My eyes focused on the numbered pages:

Page 1: The expectation to follow the Human Resources policies of the archdiocese, such as employees' wages, records, and insurance.

Page 2: The expectation to follow the policies of the archdiocese regarding the financial management of the parish, such as payroll, procedures for money counting, bookkeeping, Financial Council, bank accounts, and related matters.

Page 3: Full audit of the parish books and financial procedures by an outside agency.

I shook my head in disbelief.

"This is similar to the audit items Soller ordered for St. Barnabas! Similar opus operandi! They are playing the same game with you," I burst out in disgust. "No doubt, you're the next *kababayan* Soller is throwing under the bus!"

"According to Bishop Soller," Clem said, airing his frustration, "I needed to submit a plan in one month. The plan should specify how and when exactly the above conditions will be implemented by July 2014."

I stood up, defiant, and raised my voice. "How insensitive of them! They're quick in demanding accountability from others, yet zero from themselves." I grabbed the papers from Clem and tossed them to the side, swearing, "I can hardly wait for the day that the sacred offices those guys are occupying be replaced with worthy leaders after they're gone." I grabbed my chair, lifted it high, and banged it down on the tile floor, bursting out, "Hypocrites!"

Father Clem stood up and lightly tapped my stiff arms with his calming voice. "The officials, they come and go, but the mandate of their offices should remain sacred despite the reprehensible behavior of those occupying them. Just take it with a grain of salt."

We both sat back and held our glasses as if they were chalices. Clem stooped over his drink as if saying the prayer before communion, and then took a sip of it. I took a big gulp from mine.

"Bet you ... got ... blown ... away," I coughed out, choking over the gush of alcohol running down my throat. "Youuuu responded? To their ... expectations?"

At that, Clem sat up and spoke up as if in a courtroom, "I have answered every one of the questionnaires in all twenty-three categories. I keep records of what I have complied with. Based on the completed responses, I don't see any major violations or omissions in my parish administration."

"What do you think of your parish being audited in the first place?"

"An audit by an independent firm is most welcomed by me to erase whatever is hanging up there, impeding my immediate return from medical leave to active ministry. I hope it will take place soon. Let it be known that I am volunteering to make my presence and assistance available to the auditors to facilitate their work by clarifying matters, answering questions, and providing explanations that they needed to know about."

"Were you involved in the final stages of the audit?"

"No. I never heard from the Finance Department after I submitted my reports. By now, I figure, the audit had been completed, but I didn't get a copy of the report. I hate being put on hold." Clem made a face, turned to me, making sure I saw how he looked.

I commented on his face. "Ugly ecclesiastical clown! When can we ever get out of this charade?

"Enough of those clowning around," I said to myself, then I pursued another inquiry, "What about the decision to reinstate you?" Sounding like a sympathetic defense attorney, I stated, "California Labor Law requires the archdiocese to reinstate you as pastor, given that the medical staff already cleared your return to work."

"I brought this matter up to Bishop Soller."

"And?" I insisted on knowing more. This time, I was wearing the hat of an investigator.

"Bishop Soller keeps telling me that the archbishop is busy. I'm *still* waiting."

I paused, pondering, needing an air of relief, saying to myself, "Here we go again."

"You had other meetings with Soller? *Talaga?* Too good to be true."

"Yes, with my parish leaders," was Clem's quick response. "We verbalized our concerns to him, but he didn't seem to pay attention. Our parish leaders were so disappointed."

"Blah blah blah. Been there, done that. I'm sorry. Have you heard from the Finance Department lately? I assume you are still on that 'on hold button' delay."

"Finance Department told me that they are still working on it. Sad, it has been so long. All I needed to know is the summary of the audit report," Clem replied. He knitted his brows and asked me out of curiosity, "Do you think I'll hear from them soon? From Bishop Soller?"

"I don't think so," I replied. "I tell you, a couple of weeks ago, I asked Soller's secretary to arrange a meeting with him and me for a 'heart-to-heart' talk. Sadly, the meeting did not happen."

"Why not?" Clem curiously asked.

"Because Bishop Soller refused to meet with me in the Archdiocesan Catholic Center, which is the proper place to meet, given the nature of the subject. Rather, he insisted that the meeting should be in his office, or at one of the parishes in his region."

"What about at the golf course?" Clem suggested with a smirk.

"I don't golf, sorry. Besides, I hate being condescended upon. Again."

I raised my left foot, imagining a football player kicking a field goal to break a tie. In the act of doing so, I kicked out the words, "To meet in Soller's office means that he makes sure that the playing field is *not* level and only to his advantage. He makes sure that he has the rank advantage, his way of cloaking cowardice."

By the time we ended our conversation, we had downed the first glass of wine. We did not bother to take a second. Just being together again was more than enough to lift our spirits.

15

Fall fishing in Southern California was essentially different from summer fishing because of the targeted game fish. As has been my practice, I have been targeting surface feeders fish like calico bass and barracuda during summer and bottom-feeders like halibut and sculpin, during fall. In my experience, however, species of fish such as sharks and rays, which I know to be voracious feeders, are caught during all four seasons and are most often released. Weather, obviously, was another factor. On that day in December 2014, sunset was one hour earlier due to Pacific daylight saving time.

I had something in mind. The conversation I had with Father Clem, how badly I felt about how he felt, how I was convinced that his case and mine were interrelated, had been bothering me, so I decided to see Soller in his office.

I had my fishing attire on—Tuff fishing boots, Guy Harvey's designed T-shirt, Shimano baseball cap, Cabela's multipocket jacket, Levi's, and a pair of cutter and pointed pliers clipped on my leather belt.

"Why are you not wearing a collar?" Soller reprimanded me as I entered his office after I shut the door closed and left my rod and tackle box at the doorway. He was wearing the usual business attire of bishops. "You're not properly dressed coming to a sacred place like this," he added with a smirk.

"I'm going fishing after this stop."

"This must be a joke," Soller remarked, sneering at my outfit. "I didn't ask for you. I have a series of meetings. Come back another time. Set an appointment well in advance."

"Well in advance, huh? With me, you set appointments a day before. It happens every time."

"Have a seat," Soller said hesitatingly. He was seated on a leather chair at the head of a lacquered wood table.

Before I took the chair in front of his desk, I glanced at the large poster pinned to the wall—a photo of Pope Francis proclaiming an Extraordinary Year of Mercy. It's a picture of a smiling Pope Francis at St. Peter's Square releasing a dove whose wings were spread out, poised to take flight.

"Oh, that one," Soller commented, "I promote it here in my region. Like a good shepherd, I seek out the lost sheep."

"Church rhetoric," I said sarcastically. "The flock listens only to the authentic voice of the shepherd and follows only the one who leads them to the right path. How can you validate your claim when you run short of both?"

"Go away," Soller reacted.

"The clown that you are, I won't. Neither will my case go away. It will keep haunting you until you resolve not to do it again to other priests."

"I see my role as a support to my brother priests."

"You? A brother's keeper?" I said, taking a quick glimpse at my rod resting on the handle of the closed door. I restrained my impulse from making a flurry of imaginary casts. But I actually let go of a line of sorts, "You often speak of fraternity with priests, but all you do is pay them lip service. At times when the issues that matter most to us in our priesthood and in our priestly ministry are at hand, do you stick your out neck for us? Or do you take the easy way out, scapegoating your way up the ecclesiastical ladder?"

Silence.

In the awkwardness of silence, I glanced at my tackle box on the floor. I thought of what I had collected inside it. I recalled buying a wire leader from the local tackle shop along the way—what a good feeling. I felt protected from sharp teeth as I challenged Soller. "Do you ever practice what you preach about priestly fraternity? How do you relate this to a priest who had served faithfully for thirty-six years since ordination? Do you ever feel the pain of a pastor you removed from his parish with only five days' notice?"

"My recommendation to Archbishop Fernandez was based on consideration of the many administrative and serious financial issues of the parish, which I have been addressing with you for the past four years."

"True, but we never talked about me being removed without due process," I said.

"I did what I have to do for the sake of the better good of the church."

I blew the words out straight into Soller's face in rapid fire. "Barks but no bites. Put to practice what you preach."

I stood up to inhale a bag of air, wanting to fart it into his space. I let out, "Bull****! I flag nothing but lies in your speech. Except for the flawed reports from your henchmen in the archdiocese, you never came up with solid evidence to support your verdict."

I pulled out from one of my vest pockets a folded copy of the minutes of our parish leaders' meeting with Soller. I slapped the pages on the surface of his desk.

"Your administrative assistant, Deacon Shaeffer, took these minutes at our meeting in June 2011."

I picked up the papers, held them up, and read a critical line. "Bishop Soller then placed Father Sal Galvez on notice giving him one year to correct the administration of the parish."

I placed the pages back on the desk and pinned Soller on a line of my own.

"So why did you break your word by telling the archbishop that I should be out much sooner than what you said publicly?"

Soller pulled the crucifix out of his pocket, firmly pressing it. "Every word I say or anything I do must show my allegiance to His Grace, Archbishop Fernandez, and to His Holiness, Pope Francis," he replied in an attempt to dodge my question.

"You're not the only one pledging collaborative ministry with the archbishop," I said further, my hand hovering over the pairs of pliers clipped to my belt. "In my meeting with the archbishop last April, he told me to work together with parish leaders to address parish finances. And . . . and to follow the directives you had set with me. I followed through with every directive coming from you and your cohort in the archdiocese. And . . . and so I did with a 'yes' with regard to my meeting with the archbishop. I sent him a letter two days after the meeting."

I pulled out a page from another vest pocket. Soller reluctantly stared at it at first; then he leaned over in such a way that I thought he wanted to steal it from me.

"No, I'll read it to you," I insisted. "*Dear Archbishop, As I thank the Lord, the Good Shepherd, on the thirty-fourth anniversary of my priestly ordination, I likewise thank you, our chief shepherd, for your continued trust and support of my pastorate here at St. Barnabas. As I pledged over the years wholehearted collaborative ministry with the ordaining bishop and with his successors, I pledge my sustained collaboration with you. Likewise, as I pledged to work collaboratively with the parish leaders and the parishioners at my installation as pastor in 2004, so I also pledge to continue working with our current parish leaders and parishioners toward the vision of building up a holy and healthy parish here at St. Barnabas.*"

After I finished reading, the tragic ending of the movie *Cool Hand Luke* surreptitiously flashed in my mind. Luke, the protagonist, was convicted and sent to a forced labor camp for drunkenness and for damaging parking meters. Along with his fellow prison-fugitive, Luke sought sanctuary in a nearby church. His prayer was met only with silence. His companion betrayed him in exchange for a promise of clemency. Cornered by the pursuing sheriffs, Luke came out of hiding, his usual "cool" smile playing on his lips, mocked the sheriff captain. I balled up the page and cast it straight at Soller, quoting Luke's memorable parting line, "*What we've got here is a failure to communicate.*" It hit him squarely between his eyes.

I did not think twice before I fired more rounds of bullets.

"So, why did you not tell the archbishop that you gave the parish leaders and me a one-year deadline to work toward a balanced budget? Why did you misuse your power as a regional bishop by withholding the truth from the archbishop? You pulled a trick on him. Your backroom trickery was something unworthy of the principle we've learned in the Good Leaders, Good Shepherds Institute about leading as Jesus did."

Soller awkwardly adjusted his collar, his hands spread out to hide his dark-brown face turning pale. "I practice objective reviews and evaluations of matters brought to my attention."

I pointed a finger at him. "So, why did you say that your investigation was objective when you already excluded me?"

"So, to facilitate an independent process and to avoid possible interference from you."

"On what basis was your assertion that I was interfering with the process, one that you claimed impartial? And how could you assume that I was in the way of an objective and impartial process when you had no evidence to back up your claim? Here is where the hypocrisy of an official of the church had set in."

Silence.

At that moment, my fingers were wrapped around the handle of my fillet knife, imagining that I was drawing out the blade. I did draw a blade, of sorts, with the sharpness of piercing words. "So, you know, among professionals, objective and impartial processes are successfully carried out through the participation of all concerned parties. Common sense refutes your assertion of my interference in the process, given that I was already excluded from it—*if ever there was a process at all.*"

Soller's face had now turned pale.

"You really are a bully," I said as I turned to leave.

Dead silence.

I gazed westward. The sun had already set.

16

Pope Francis's visit to the Philippines on January 14–19, 2015, was one of his unique ways of bringing the light of faith to the people of God. His mission was to show the compassion of Jesus to the Filipino people, especially to those victims of natural calamities.

Like a lighthouse, he beamed a glow of hope and comfort to the land on the east side of the Pacific that had just suffered a very high number of lives lost and massive devastation. The super typhoon, Yolanda, had hit the Philippines in October of the previous year. It was the strongest typhoon ever recorded in history. It damaged hundreds of thousands of houses and destroyed the populations' means of livelihood.

I was so blessed to concelebrate in the late-morning mass presided by Pope Francis in the Immaculate Conception Cathedral in Manila on January 16th. Approximately 2,000 bishops, priests, and religious participated. The gospel (Jn. 21:15–17) was about the dialogue between the risen Lord and Peter. The Lord asked Peter thrice if he loved Him, to which Peter responded yes thrice. The Holy Father started his homily with "Do you love me?" to which we, the priests and the religious, responded in a deafening "yes." Our resounding "yesses" did not surprise Pope Francis, but he reminded us that Jesus continues to accept us in spite of our weaknesses.

January 17 was a stormy day, signal #2 of typhoon Amang. Pope Francis, wearing a yellow raincoat, presided at the mass in Tacloban City. Approximately 200,000 rain-soaked faithful participated in the service. Many of those in the crowd were survivors of the super-typhoon, Yolanda, which took the lives of about 10,000, along with 3,000 missing residents.

In his homily, the pope said, in part, "So many of you have lost everything. I don't know what to say to you, but the Lord does know what to say to you. Some of you lost part of your families. All I can do is keep silent, and I walk with you all with my silent heart." Hundreds of thousands of worshippers wiped the tears under the hoods of their yellow raincoats as the Holy Father spoke those words of comfort.

In an analogous way, the strongest emotional, psychological, and spiritual typhoon that ever hit my priesthood was my removal from St. Barnabas parish. It was not the super typhoon Yolanda's wind up to 200 miles per hour, nor its floodwaters of up to twenty feet high. It was the giant, venomous, five-headed snake of lack of communication, of insensitivity to the people of God, of the inconsistency of expectation, of poor leadership, and of unethical work ethic long exhibited by church leaders in the Archdiocese of Los Arboles that had bitten me.

I was uprooted from St. Barnabas parish by the vicious recommendation of Soller and by the detached concurrence of Fernandez. However, they did not succeed in uprooting my cultural roots. As a boy growing up in the Philippines, I planted bamboo. I cheered them as they grew tall, delighting on the multiplicity of their usefulness—stringed bamboos made for rafts, and their twigs for fishing poles. Bamboo bent against furious storms, but they didn't break. Their resiliency taught and prepared me to weather storms that raged across my priesthood.

On the morning of the next day, Pope Francis presided at the "Encounter with the Youth" event held at the University of Santo Tomas. About 30,000 youths from all over the country took part in the event. The Holy Father showed mercy and compassion to the young people, the future of the church and the world. One of the youth representatives was Glyzelle Palomar, a twelve-year-old orphan rescued from the streets of Manila. Her eyes, wet with tears, and her voice, the voice of an abandoned child, asked the pope why so many innocent people suffer and why so few help them. The Holy Father hugged her, responding, "Certain realities in life can only be seen through eyes cleansed by tears." As I watched, I too felt the warm embrace of the Holy Father. I imagined him whispering in my ear, "You are not alone in your sorrows." And to the question why God allows suffering, the Holy Father assured Glyzelle and millions of television viewers, me included, that the only worthy answer to it is through tears of compassion. In the background, a huge banner hanging from a high-rise building with the words "*Maraming salamat, Papa Francisco, sa inyong pagmamalasakit*" (Thank you, Pope Francis, for your compassion) caught my attention. As deeply as the message pierced my heart, it quickly brought tears to my eyes.

Pope Francis had designated the coming year as the Extraordinary Jubilee Year of Mercy. The theme was "Merciful as the Father." He reminded me that to be merciful means to enter into the other person's sufferings. I have to feel the other person's pain, see through the other person's eyes, and place myself inside the other person's heart and mind. With recurring thoughts of having been thrown out of St. Barnabas parish and feeling thrown out of my house, I made up my mind that it was only through compassion, *pagmamalasakit*, that the culture of sacred silence could disintegrate. That night, I decided that upon my return to Los Angeles, I'd work on the details of the local council of the Knights of Columbus in collaboration with the Make-A-Wish Foundation to sponsor a day of fishing for boys and girls who were terminally ill.

Once again, I was so blessed to be one of the concelebrants at the concluding mass presided by Pope Francis at Luneta Park in Manila on January 18, 2015. It was another stormy day. Pope Francis once again wore a yellow raincoat on top of his vestments. In spite of the pouring rain and cold wind coming from Manila Bay, the people stayed for hours to attend the mass.

Pope Francis, who came from the "ends of the earth," following the guiding star of his faith, encountered the faith of the Filipino people. At the mass where an estimated six million people participated, a possible all-time record for the most mass attendance in the history of the Catholic Church, the pope praised the strong faith of the Filipino people, along with their resiliency and close family ties. I rejoiced at the thought that I was counted among the many who were blessed with both faith and family.

After the celebration of the mass, the rites of candle lighting and mission-sending were performed. I joined the millions of others in attendance with our lit candles held up high, and I listened attentively as the narration was read:

"In the beginning, the universe was dark and cold—and the Spirit hovered and brooded and whispered: 'Let there be life! Let there be light!'

"The light passed on to those who sought to understand God's creation—and explored its wonders. The light passed to those who saw the dignity of human beings and fought to bring justice to the poor—freedom to those who were slaves.

"Who will keep the light burning in our day? Who will take the light into the world? Who will carry the light—if we do not? Who will carry the light—if you do not?"

The rites concluded with the words of Pope Francis, "My dear brothers and sisters, we received this light in baptism and were entrusted with keeping this light burning brightly. We vowed to spread this light when we were confirmed. I ask you now: Keep the flame of faith alive in your hearts. Walk always as children of the light. This is the mission of every Christian."

By the time Pope Francis was leaving Luneta Park on the Jeep Popemobile, having made several rounds blessing the people and kissing babies, the deafening cheers of the crowd "*Lolo Kiko, mahal kayo ng Pilipino*" (Grandpa Francis, the Filipino people love you) filled the air, breaking through the dark clouds overhead. The flames from the million candles, not extinguished by the wind blowing from Manila Bay, were bright enough to ease the gloom of the encroaching storm.

I swiped away a tear rolling down my cheek as I watched the open-top Popemobile leave Luneta Park. Millions of hands waving goodbye to the pope were like hands waving away the gloom in my heart, the gloom of the storm that enveloped me since my removal from St. Barnabas. The light of faith that Pope Francis brought from Rome partly eased the darkness that clericalism in the Archdiocese of Los Arboles had encircled me with.

The next day, Pope Francis traveled back to Rome, inspired by the light of the million candles, the collective faith of the Filipino people. I returned to Los Angeles, inspired by the light of *one* additional candle . . . Pope Francis.

17

I was standing on the shore along the Long Beach Harbor that night, two weeks after I returned from the Philippines. The telegraphic light beams from Angel's Gate Lighthouse kept me company in the dark. Earbuds plugged to my phone's iTunes piped music from Simon and Garfunkel's *Sound of Silence*. The song conveyed to me the truth that many people do talk but don't speak, hear but don't listen because they refuse to disturb the sound of silence.

"You must be crazy," Raul exclaimed, his voice breaking the silence at the beach and wafting toward the surf. He arrived a few minutes later to the spot where I told him I'd be surf-fishing. "I said, you must be out of your mind." Raul held my forearm, shaking my attention off the music. I turned the music off and quickly unplugged the earbuds.

The evening high tide was building up. The roaring waves pounded the shoreline so loud I could hardly hear Raul's voice sounding as if he were laying a guilt trip on me. "I came because you asked me to be here. I'm not used to fishing in the dark. Definitely, not a good idea."

I ignored Raul's interference. He shouted straight to my ears, "What are you doing? What do you catch at night?"

"I call it poetic fishing," I replied, firing away the surface jig into the dark vastness of the Pacific Ocean. "Fishing is not just catching fish," I went on, saying as I reeled the jig in to cast again. "It's about the power to unleash one's potential to make a little difference . . . sort of . . . in our archdiocese."

"Woo . . . hoo . . . Are you serious?"

"Deaddd se-rioussss," I replied, casting out my line again.

The splash of the jig hitting the surface of the water was subsequently diminished by the giant splash of a creature that just took the sardine-shaped lure, taking it deep down as it took line off the reel. The reel smoked as it fed taut monofilament to the demanding pressure at the end of the line. I adjusted the drag to modulate the rapid uncoiling of the line. I set the hook, then cranked the reel handle about ten revolutions. I felt an unyielding resistance determined to break the line. I tipped the rod to put pressure on the creature to turn it toward my direction. Then I placed the rod butt into the rod holder tied around my waist and cranked harder and faster. Slowly, I recovered a foot of line.

"Hook up!" I yelled at the top of my lungs, calculating that the treble hooks had solidly embedded in the corner of the creature's mouth. Then I called out, "It's a shark!" fearing that the creature would bite off the wire leader. "Raul, go get the hand gaff."

"How do you know it's a shark and not a halibut?" Raul hollered as he picked up the retractable gaff from my tackle box.

"Not a halibut," I hollered back. "I don't feel a sharp head shake."

The creature breached out of the water, shaking the jig off its mouth. I took a few strides out into the water, up to my waist, holding the tip of my rod up as it bent under pressure. The line kept peeling off thinner and further out into the black water. I tightened the drag a bit more so I wouldn't get spooled.

Momentarily, I felt less tension at the end of the line, so I cranked the reel handle as fast as I could so I could turn the fish toward me. But then, again, the reel started whirring as the fish dove deep, pulling me deeper into the water. I replaced the rod butt under my armpit since the water level had passed my waist. I cranked faster and pulled harder. Under more pressure, the fish surged, violently shaking the jig off its mouth. When it surfaced above the waterline, its recognizable colors showed.

"Looks like a juvenile blue shark!" I announced excitedly.

"Release it," Raul ordered. He dropped the gaff on the sand.

"I won't."

"But why? Shark fillets don't taste good."

"Scavengers that they are, I don't throw back." I stood my ground.

I kept reeling in. I felt less resistance though the weight was wearing my arms out. "Which means . . . one less predator . . . in this wide ocean . . . such as . . . in the Archdiocese of Los Arboles," I interjected, gasping for breath between phrases.

"But why?" Raul sounded like a wrecking ball hit him.

"As in Soller's case, it's easy to fall into a habit of preying on subordinates." I kept reeling in as fast as I could. I gained more line in. "Releasing him . . . increases the likelihood of him . . . preying on others."

By now, my arms were giving up.

"Raul," I yelled for assistance, "your turn." I handed the rod to him. He took it after a bit of hesitation. "Crank . . . crank . . . crank . . ." I ordered. "Keep the rod tip up. Don't give it a chance to turn its head. Keep cranking till it comes knee-deep." Raul struggled fighting the shark as it vigorously pumped its tail against the shallow water. With lighning speed, I ran to pick up the gaff on the sand.

Armed with the fully extended gaff, its sharp jay hook exposed,

I charged the water. Both hands firmly pressed on its rubberized tubular aluminum handle, I sank its large hook deep into the shark's lower jaw. On contact, the shark made a series of wild pumps on the water, alternating with its shudders on the surface. Salt sprayed in my eyes, the shark's blood squirted straight to my face. A high tide undertow hit my limbs, and I lost my footing but didn't lose my hold on the gaff. An alloy of water and blood meridian marked the duel zone for the fisherman and the fish.

With my left hand still holding on to the shaking gaff, my right reached for the pair of pliers clipped to my belt, and I stabbed the shark's head with its pointed tip, keeping the pliers deeply embedded there. Then I grabbed the other pair of pliers, a wire cutter, and cut the line off the fish, leaving the jig dangling at the corner of its mouth, below the razor-sharp rows of its teeth.

"Let it go," Raul ordered again. "It's just like a baby. Please."

I ignored his plea.

As I dragged the creature out of the water, its tail slapped the sand along the shoreline, tossing grains into the air. From its head oozed a mucus of light red and gray; from its mouth, steady drops of fluid, dripping through the dangling iron lure, and dropping spots of dark red along the path.

As soon as I reached the spot of the hookup, I unhooked the gaff, folded it, and tossed it into my opened tackle box. I pulled my fillet knife from my right hand hip belt. I buried its blade first in the creature's right eye, and then, to its left, meticulously gouging both eyes. Secure in my hands, now bloodied and dripping, the creature's eyeballs, a roundish shape like jiggling jelly looked up to the heavens. They seemed to be crying out, "Let this sacrifice be an offering acceptable to you . . . for the forgiveness of sins."

Then I fell on my knees, shaking but holding firm on what I had in the palm of my hand.

"Stand up," Raul's voice was firm, his hands pulling me up. "You're out of your mind, and I'm getting sick."

I ignored him again.

I dropped the bloody pair to free my hands. My tainted knife poised for more action, I turned the creature over with my foot as I ran my hand over its belly, saying to myself, "Poor thing, but you must go." Then, lightning fast and in a single swipe of the blade, I slashed open its belly. To my wild surprise, amniotic fluid flowed out, flushing along tiny shapes of their mother's resemblance, recognizable by their dark eyes and rubbery bodies . . . about a dozen of them.

"You made me believe it's a juvenile," Raul's voice loaded with guilt echoed along the shoreline. "Now, for the last time, I urge you to let the babies go."

"No," I said firmly. "They'll do what their ancestors did before them."

Raul threw up.

In the spur of the moment, I dug deeper into the creature's entrails and searched for its heart. Feeling the beating dynamo in my hand, I ripped it off its rib-protected shield and its electrically charged conduits. With both hands, I squeezed it to extract warmth from it and to transfuse it to my being. Blood swirling and gurgling in the hollow of the palms of my hand, I smeared it on my face. Drops of blood flowing down, forming minute puddles on my dimples, snaking alongside my neck veins, and ultimately, staining my clothes.

Angel's Lighthouse beams of light warmed me up in the cold of the night.

It was then that I realized that I was not the sacrificial victim any longer, but Aaron and Christ, the high priests at the altar of sacrifice.

"Hu...hu...hu..." Raul sighed, one hand wiping off vomit from his mouth, his other hand nursing his stomach. "Are you doing more of this?"

Quietly, I walked over to the spot to pick up my rod.

"But how can you . . .? Raul trailed off. ". . . fish again . . . with so much violence?"

I pointed the tip of the rod toward the direction of Angel's Gate Lighthouse.

"Oh yes . . ." Raul exclaimed, his eyes beaming. ". . . by the light of faith."

With a stirring new voice inside of me, I placed the palms of my hands on the sides of my mouth, and I shouted at the top of my lungs into the vastness of the horizon, "Tomorrow's a new day!"

"What do you mean by that?" he asked.

"The Knights of Columbus and I will be taking the group of terminally ill kids for a day of fishing. Their parents said they had only a few days to live."

Raul's curiosity escalated. "Why? Why them?"

"Mercy. A bit of mercy makes the world less cold and more just," I recited in a loud voice, quoting Pope Francis.

I retied the jig, paying no attention to its chewed-up shape and crooked treble hooks. I cast my line one more time with so much enthusiasm, inspired by Pope Francis's call for a radical change of heart. He said it in Rome a few days after my sixty-second birthday, I recalled. I reeled the line in, ignoring the surface jig's erratic swimming motion, mimicking a wounded sardine. I lifted the rod, feeling the jig dangle off its tip. Then I pulled out my pliers, cut the jig off, and threw it into my tackle box. I heard the clink of the jig as it fell among the heap of iron. I closed my tackle box, lamenting that a year after Pope Francis's call to the universal church to be merciful, the Archdiocese of Los Arboles removed me from St. Barnabas.

Raul and I said good night to each other. One hand carrying the tackle box, and the other, clutching the rod, I walked a few steps toward the spot where my car was parked. Squinting at the streak of light from Angel's Gate Lighthouse, I called out to Raul, who was heading to his car parked in another section of the beach, "You are right. *Those guys* . . . They really screwed me up." I took several steps in his direction. "I know you are disgusted with the way I dealt with the mother shark and her babies. Sorry."

Raul halted, turned around, then took several steps toward me. "By the way, have you heard the latest news?" he asked in his usual way of talking, trailed off, and mimicked a stutter, "Va-va-ti-cannn Nnnew-newss says Biss-biss-bishop So-so-sol-lerrrr mo-mo-moved, ass-ass-assigned to an-an-another di-dio-cese." I could tell that he was a happy camper by the way he spoke.

"*Promovetur ut moveatur*," I recited in response. I shifted my gaze from the lighthouse's streak of light to the blackened horizon. "Latin for 'to kick up so to kick out.' Somehow, our voices crying out for justice and mercy had reached the ears of Pope Francis. Somehow, our letters, those from St. Perpetua's, especially the one sent to the Apostolic Nuncio in Washington, did the trick."

"I see," Raul surmised, flashing a two thumbs-up sign. "You're right too," he added. "Much more fun fishing in the dark."

18

The week after, a sunny day, which was typical of a Southern California winter, the sport fisher *Independence* took us - twenty-one kids, five officers of Knights of Columbus, and two reps from Make-A-Wish Foundation for a day of fishing off Long Beach Harbor. As part of its program, every year at this time, Make-A-Wish Foundation chartered a fishing boat for terminally ill youths whose last wish was to spend a day fishing.

The Knights of Columbus and I collaborated with Make-A-Wish Foundation to take Alejandro, a fourth-grader from a Las Colinas public school who was diagnosed with leukemia, and the other children in similar medical conditions. As the beneficiaries of the Make-A-Wish Foundation and with the funds raised by the Knights of Columbus, Alejandro and all the others received a new Shimano rod and reel combo, which they used for the first time, targeting bottom-feeders such as sculpins, sand dabs, and flounders.

All aboard, packed with an excited group of youthful fisher boys and girls and with us, their adult chaperones, the sport fisher was on its way to a Disneyland at sea. The skipper turned the ignition key on, the boat's twin engines roared, and the propellers engaged. We headed to the fishing spot called the "Rigs," so named after the six oil rig structures, about an hour's boat ride from the dock. Minutes later, after the boat had cleared Long Beach Harbor, Angel's Gate Lighthouse at the end of breakwater loomed in front of us. Alejandro and the rest of the group, who I guessed had not seen it before, rushed to the bow of the boat to have a good view of it.

"You're not gonna leave home without it," the skipper, who noted the wide-eyed young anglers' admiration of the towering lighthouse, came on the PA system from his spot on the bridge. "You sure needin' it coming home," he added, reminding the curious youngsters of the guiding role of the lighthouse.

We had arrived at the Rigs. Then the skipper announced, "Go get 'em, boys and girls." Every boy and girl got into action, so excited to use their new gear, ignoring their flailing physical conditions, summoning up their inner energy, too anxious to get their line in the water for a catch. The skipper, the two deckhands, the Knights of Columbus, and Make-A-Wish Foundation chaperones stationed themselves in several spots of the boat to assist the boys and girls as they fished all day.

I walked a few feet toward the stern to assist Alejandro. I stopped by the bait tank to scoop a lively anchovy and tossed it to him to catch. He missed, but quickly picked it up on the deck.

"Your catch of the day," I quipped.

While we stood, leaning on the stern's wooden rail, pitifully watching the wiggling bait on Alejandro's open palm, I commented, "It will survive only if you know how to handle it well. But for now, it's your *bait*."

I instructed him how to nose-hook it, to carefully avoid hooking through its eyes to keep it swimming naturally as it hits the water. "Bottom-feeders love live bait," I commented.

"*But I want it to live*," Alejandro protested.

"We came here to fish," I said in a reprimand. "You can't catch anything without bait."

Alejandro ignored me. In no time, he picked up the anchovy with his other hand, kissed it goodbye, and tossed it over the rail. It hit the water and swam freely. "*Hasta la vista, 'migo*," he bade the bait fish goodbye, waving as the fish swam deep into the water.

We silently watched the anchovy merge into its brand-new water world. Then Alejandro turned to me, his face lit up, a big smile played on his lips, and said, "Awesome day!" In that mystical moment, I heard him say to me, "*I wanna be free*. Just like that lively bait." At that very moment, I choked up at the thought that it could be the last time Alejandro went fishing. I knew then I wouldn't see him or hear from him again.

From then on, I keep longing for Alejandro's face to shine at times in my dark hours, his smiles in cold nights, his voice - persuasive and compassionate - to warm my heart. His last wish, an affirmation of life itself, touches me to the core, challenges me to keep moving on, better yet, *inspires* me to be my best.